a **MISFITZ** mystery

The
ONe THat goT Away

Josh Lacey was born in London. He is the eldest of seven children. He now lives in London with his wife and their daughter.

He worked as a journalist, a screenwriter and a teacher before publishing his first novel for children, A Dog Called Grk.

You can find out more about him and his books at www.joshlacey.com.

Also by Josh Lacey

Bearkeeper

Writing as Joshua Doder

The Grk Series

A Dog Called Grk
Grk and the Pelotti Gang
Grk and the Hot Dog Trail
Grk: Operation Tortoise
Grk Smells a Rat
Grk Takes Revenge

Praise for *Bearkeeper*

"A highly enjoyable read"
Guardian

"*Bearkeeper* informs as it entertains
and intrigues as it enlightens"
FT

"Boys of 9+ will love Josh Lacey's *Bearkeeper*. . .
The humour and wisdom of his tale will win
[the author] new fans"
The Times

"There is enough here to keep readers glued to
the page and to provide them with an enthralling
introduction to 17th-century England"
Books for Keeps

"A most engaging and powerfully dramatic
adventure. . . We recommend it firmly"
Bookbag

a MISFITZ mystery

The One That Got Away

JOSH LACEY

MARION LLOYD BOOKS

First published in the UK in 2009 by Marion Lloyd Books
An imprint of Scholastic Ltd
Euston House, 24 Eversholt Street
London, NW1 1DB, UK
Registered office: Westfield Road, Southam,
Warwickshire, CV47 0RA
SCHOLASTIC and associated logos are trademarks and/or
registered trademarks of Scholastic Inc.

ISBN 9781407105444

A CIP catalogue record for this book
is available from the British Library

Printed in the UK by CPI Bookmarque, Croydon, CR0 4TD
Papers used by Scholastic Children's Books are made
from wood grown in sustainable forests.

3 5 7 9 10 8 6 4

www.scholastic.co.uk/zone

To Bella

1

Ben was woken at 5.25 in the morning. He shoved his hand under the pillow and felt for his phone. He'd set it on silent, so the alarm vibrated through the pillow, interrupting his sleep without making any noise.

He pressed a key to switch it off.

He sat up slowly and peered over the edge of his bed, looking down at the bottom bunk. There was a lump under the duvet. It didn't move. It carried on not moving. Frank was still asleep.

Dawn wasn't for another ten minutes, but slim chinks of light were already sneaking through the curtains. Ben knew he didn't have any time to waste. If he was going to catch the thief, he had to do it now.

He pushed aside the duvet, slid out of bed and climbed down the ladder, trying not to make any noise.

The floorboards felt cold against his bare feet.

Ben had slept in his T-shirt and boxer shorts, ready for an early start, and left his jeans, socks and trainers in a neat pile on a chair. He bundled them into his arms and tiptoed across the room. Dressing downstairs would make much less noise. He opened the door, glanced once more at Frank, checking he hadn't woken up, then went into the corridor.

He closed the door behind him and listened for a few seconds.

If his mum or his sisters had woken up, he would have heard their voices or their footsteps, but the house was quiet. They were still asleep.

Ben padded along the corridor and down the stairs. In the hallway, he pulled on his clothes, then crouched on the icy flagstones to tie up his shoes.

He opened the front door. The cold air grabbed the bare skin of his face and arms. He should have worn a jumper. Too late now. Maybe the air would warm up when the sun rose.

Pulling the door shut behind him, he walked into the front garden and had a pee against the stone wall. He hadn't wanted to use the loo upstairs in case the noise woke anyone.

Birds flitted between the trees that surrounded the cottage. In the sky, a few wispy clouds were catching the first rays of the rising sun. Ben didn't often take much notice of nature, but this was beautiful. He should have brought a camera.

No time to worry about that now.

He walked round the side of the cottage, opened the gate and went into the vegetable garden.

There was no one to be seen. The garden looked the same as yesterday. Nothing had been disturbed.

Ben walked to a patch of grass at the far end of the garden and sat down. It was the perfect spot. As soon as someone came into the garden, he would see them.

He might have to hang around for an hour. Maybe even two. But he didn't mind. He'd stay all day if he had to.

He leaned back against the fence and settled down for a long wait.

When he opened his eyes, the sun had risen above the trees.

Hours must have passed. He had fallen asleep.

I'm an idiot, thought Ben. What kind of detective falls asleep in the middle of a stake-out?

Someone could have come and taken everything and he wouldn't even have noticed.

He sat up and looked around, checking to see if anything had changed.

That was when he saw the thief.

2

Four days earlier, Ben had been waiting for his brother.

Actually, that's not quite true. Ben didn't have a brother. He had a stepbrother and a half-brother. Between them, they didn't quite add up to a whole brother.

That afternoon, he was waiting for his stepbrother.

He was standing on the platform of a small railway station in a quiet country town. His two sisters, Harmony and Kitkat, were beside him.

The three of them had been there for several minutes, watching the empty tracks, searching for the first signs of the train from Bristol, when Kitkat said, "Do you think we'll recognize him?"

"Yes," said Ben.

"How do you know?"

"We saw him at Christmas. People don't change in seven months."

"He might have."

"He won't."

"People do change a lot, you know," said Kitkat. "Remember when Uncle Barnaby came back from Africa with a bone through his. . ." She paused in mid-sentence and put her head on one side. Then she said, "There it is."

"There's what?" said Ben.

"The train."

"How do you know?"

"I can hear it."

"I can't," said Ben. But as soon as those words left his mouth, he heard the distant roar of the engine. A moment later, he caught his first glimpse of the train through the trees.

Approaching the platform, the train slowed and shuddered to a halt. Doors swung open. Passengers poured out, carrying books and newspapers and handbags and briefcases. Some hurried towards the exit. Others greeted the people who had been waiting for them. Husbands hugged their wives. Boyfriends snogged their girlfriends. A little girl cried "Daddy!" and jumped into a tall man's arms.

And there was Frank.

A scrawny boy was sauntering along the platform. He had a rucksack slung over his shoulder. He was wearing black jeans, black socks, black plimsolls, a black T-shirt and a pair of black-rimmed glasses.

Ben nudged his little sister. "You see?"

"OK, OK," said Kitkat. "You were right."

Frank stopped opposite his siblings and stared at them with a curious expression, as if he had the sense that he had seen them somewhere before, but he couldn't quite remember where or when.

Harmony was the oldest so she spoke first. "Hello, Frank," she said. "How are you?"

"Fine," said Frank.

"How was the trip?" said Harmony.

"Fine."

"The train's a bit late," said Harmony.

Frank nodded, but didn't speak.

Harmony, Ben and Kitkat stood there for a moment, waiting for Frank to say something, anything, till they realized he wasn't going to. And then Harmony said, "Mum's waiting in the car. This way."

She turned and walked towards the exit.

Frank followed a few paces behind.

Ben and Kitkat glanced at one another. Kitkat raised her eyebrows as if to say: *What a freak, huh?* Ben grinned in agreement. And they hurried after the others.

3

Jennifer Fitzroy was a tall, slim woman with long brown hair and sharp green eyes. She was elegantly dressed in a black skirt and a white silk blouse. A necklace of shimmering jade hung around her neck. She was standing in the middle of the carpark with an open book in one hand and a pencil in the other, scribbling notes in the margin as she read.

When she saw her stepson emerging from the door of the station, accompanied by her son and her daughters, she hurried forward, her arms outstretched.

"Frank," she cried. "How lovely to see you!"

She wrapped her arms around his body and squeezed him in a tight embrace.

Frank allowed himself to be hugged, but his own arms stayed rigidly by his sides. From the expression on his face, you might have guessed that he had just bitten into the flesh of a lemon.

Finally, Jennifer released him. "How was the train?"

"Fine," said Frank.

"Good. Now, let's go and find the house. Hop in, darlings. Will you all fit?"

The car was tightly packed with bags, boxes, books, games, towels, toys, tins of beans, packets of pasta and just about everything else that a family of five could possibly need during a month's holiday in the countryside. Jennifer and Harmony sat in the front. Ben and Frank squeezed into the back with Kitkat between them.

Doors slammed. Jennifer started the engine. And they were off.

They drove out of the station carpark and headed into the countryside. On either side of the road, fields of swaying corn stretched to the horizon.

No one spoke. Jennifer concentrated on driving. Harmony stared at the map spread across her knees. Frank and Kitkat listened to their iPods. Ben looked out of the window and wondered when he would be old enough to skip family holidays and do something more interesting instead.

After fifteen or twenty minutes, they came to a left turn signposted to Chadwick.

"That's it," said Harmony.

"I know," said Jennifer. "I've been here before. So have you, actually, but you were too small to remember."

She turned left. The road soon narrowed, but luckily they didn't meet another car. They entered some thick woods. On their right, there was a high wall. Signs nailed into the bricks warned that this was PRIVATE PROPERTY and visitors should KEEP OUT or the GUARD DOGS would get them.

When they had been driving through the woods for about five minutes, Jennifer stopped the car opposite a wooden gate. On the other side of the gate, a rough track wound through the trees.

They followed the track and came to a little white cottage with a grey slate roof.

Quarryman's Cottage was originally built to house a family who worked in the nearby quarry. It had three rooms downstairs – a kitchen, a sitting-room and a study – and three bedrooms upstairs.

Jennifer took the biggest bedroom, and Harmony and Kitkat shared the smaller one, leaving the tiny room at the back of the house for Ben and Frank.

*

The two boys carried their bags into their bedroom and stood in the doorway, staring at the bunk bed crammed against the back wall. The bed took up most of the room, allowing just enough space for a chest of drawers and some shelves.

At home, Ben's bedroom was twice the size. And he had it all to himself.

He turned to Frank. "Which bunk do you want? Up or down?"

"Don't care," said Frank.

"You can choose. You're the guest."

"Like I said, I don't care."

"We'll toss a coin." Ben reached into his pocket and took out a ten-pence piece. "Heads or tails?"

"Don't care."

"You can have heads, then." Ben tossed the coin and caught it in his palm. "Sorry. Tails." He held his hand out to prove he hadn't cheated, but Frank didn't even bother looking.

Ben pocketed the coin and took the better bunk, the top one.

If I was a nicer person, thought Ben, I'd give this bunk to Frank. He's the guest. But why should I? Did I ask to share a room with him?

Ben dumped his bag in the middle of the bed,

undid the zip and tipped out the contents, making a big pile of shirts, socks, pants, books and comics. He considered unpacking properly, putting his stuff on the shelves, but decided not to bother. He leaned over the side of the bed and looked down to see what his stepbrother was doing.

On the bottom bunk, Frank was opening his own bag and pulling out a sleek black laptop. He flipped the lid.

Ben said, "Is that yours?"

"Yes."

"I bet it was expensive."

Frank nodded, but didn't say anything. He just stared at the screen through the thick lenses of his black-rimmed glasses.

"Mum wouldn't let me bring mine," said Ben. "She said the whole point of going to the countryside is not having things like phones and computers."

Frank started typing fast. He didn't appear to have heard anything that Ben had said.

Ben stayed there for a moment, staring at Frank, feeling like an idiot. Then he grabbed a random book from the pile on his bunk, scurried down the ladder and headed for the door.

He went outside, lay on the grass and opened the book. He didn't really feel like reading, but anything was better than staying in the same room as Frank, pretending not to be interested in whatever he was doing.

4

That summer, Frank's mother had gone to India. Frank didn't want to go, and his mum never forced him to do anything that he didn't want to, so she asked Jeremy and Jennifer if he could stay with them at Quarryman's Cottage.

"Of course he can," Jennifer said. "It'll be a chance for all the kids to get to know one another better."

Ben said: I don't want to get to know Frank better. I know enough about him already.

He never talks. He never smiles. He just sits there with his headphones over his ears, listening to his freaky music and staring at you with his freaky eyes.

I don't want to see him. I don't want to talk to him. And I definitely don't want to share my personal space with him.

If he has to come with us, couldn't he sleep in a tent in the garden?

Actually, Ben didn't say any of these things. He knew there was no point. Whether he liked it or not, he was going to have to spend a month in the country sharing a room with Frank the freak.

5

Sometimes people asked Ben to explain how he was related to the rest of his family. And then they wished they hadn't.

He always said, "Shall I draw a diagram?"

"Oh, no," they replied. "You needn't do that. Just explain it."

So he did.

At first, people were fascinated. Then they were puzzled. Finally they shook their heads and asked him to stop, saying they were completely confused.

"Don't worry," Ben would say. "I find it confusing too. Why don't I draw a diagram?"

Drawing a diagram, he had discovered, was the easiest way to explain how his family fitted together.

On a piece of paper, he wrote the names of his parents and his siblings. He drew lines between them, showing the relationships that connected him to his mother, his father, his sister, his half-sister, his half-brother, his stepbrother, his stepbrother's mother, his father's girlfriend and his mother's husband.

Looking at the diagram, people usually smiled and said something like, "Wow, you certainly have a big family."

"That's right," said Ben. "One big happy family."

From his tone of voice, people could never tell whether he was joking or serious, and none of them ever asked.

Here is one of the family trees that Ben drew:

BEN'S FAMILY

Celia ← New Girlfriend

Martha
Never Actually Married
American
Dead

Dad
Robot Arms

Dutch
my brother
no one knows
where he is

Mum
Jennifer
Fitzroy

Divorced
Ages Ago

Married

Jeremy
Fitzroy
my stepfather

Also Divorced
Ages Ago

Nina
lives in
Bristol

Frank
my step brother

Harmony
my sister

ME

Kit Kat
the youngest

If you didn't count Dutch, and they usually didn't, because they'd never met him and weren't even sure he existed, Harmony was the oldest of the siblings. She was reliable, responsible, careful, practical and twelve. Without her, the whole family would have fallen to pieces. That was what Harmony thought, anyway, and she was probably right.

Frank came next. He was a tall, skinny boy with long limbs and messy black hair. He always wore the same clothes: black jeans, black socks, black plimsolls, a black T-shirt and a pair of black-rimmed glasses. He lived with his mother in Bristol. Three or four times a year, he came to stay with his father's new family in London, but he never said very much and the others knew hardly anything about him.

Ben was a month younger than Frank. And slightly smaller. But he changed his clothes more often.

Ben's younger sister was seven. Her full name was Katherine Daisy Venetia Fitzroy, but no one ever called her anything but Kitkat. She was the baby of the family and took full advantage of that fact. If you have a baby sister – or are lucky enough to be one yourself – you'll know exactly what I mean.

6

They soon settled into a routine.

Every morning, after breakfast, Jennifer went into her study and closed the door. She sat at the desk by the window and typed fast. She was determined to finish her book by the end of the month.

Jennifer and Jeremy had planned to come to the cottage together. While she was writing, he could have spent some quality time with the children. The five of them would have gone on expeditions together, walking in the hills, driving to the sea, visiting local monuments and exploring the countryside. At the last minute, Jeremy had been invited to Beijing for a conference. He would be back for the final week of the holiday.

The children didn't mind. They were used to taking care of themselves.

Harmony did all the cooking and the housework, sometimes doling out basic tasks to the others or writing shopping lists for her mother. She couldn't do the shopping herself, because Quarryman's Cottage was miles from the nearest town. Even the nearest village was more than an hour's walk away. Harmony knew how to drive, but wasn't allowed to. She'd been taught by her dad when she last stayed with him in Los Angeles. As soon as she reached her seventeenth birthday, she was planning to pass her test and buy a car. For now, she had to hand a shopping list to her mother and send her to the supermarket.

Kitkat was teaching herself to be a pop star. When she wasn't looking at the latest issue of *Heat* or *Grazia*, she'd sit in the garden with her iPod, learning songs, practising the words and the tunes till she got them precisely right.

Frank stayed in his bedroom with his computer and his headphones, emerging only to eat, drink and go to the loo. No one knew what he was doing and no one asked.

As for Ben . . .

. . . well, Ben wasn't quite sure how he managed to get from the morning to the evening without dying of boredom.

When he complained to his mother, she wasn't exactly sympathetic.

"You can't be bored," said Jennifer. "There's so much to do here."

"Like what?"

"You could go for a walk." Jennifer gestured out of the window at the glorious landscape surrounding the cottage. The lawn was glistening in the sunlight. Birds were singing and a gentle breeze ruffled the leaves in the trees. If you were the type of person who liked yomping through fields, swinging your arms and drawing deep draughts of clean air into your lungs, the sight would have filled you with wild excitement.

Ben wasn't that type of person. "I don't feel like walking," he said.

"What do you feel like doing?"

"Going home."

"You know that isn't an option," said Jennifer. "Why don't you play a game with your sisters?"

"They're boring."

"Your brother, then."

"He's not my brother."

"He's your stepbrother. And you could make an effort to be nice to him. You don't see him very often."

"I don't want to be nice to him," said Ben. "I don't like him."

Jennifer sighed. "You're being very difficult today. Are you depressed?"

"No."

"Is there anything you want to talk about?"

"No."

"Are you sure, Benjy? If you want to talk, I'm always ready to listen. You know that, don't you?"

"Yes, Mum."

"I've got a good idea. Why don't you read a book?"

"I'm bored of reading."

"You'd better find something to do," said Jennifer, picking up her coffee. "We're going to be here for a month. You can't be bored every day or you'll drive everyone insane. Now, I've got to do some work or I'll fall behind schedule." She leaned down, kissed Ben on the cheek, then hurried to her study, calling over her shoulder: "See you later, darling. Have a lovely day!"

Holidays, thought Ben.

I hate them.

Actually, that wasn't quite true. He liked holidays at home. He liked sleeping late and playing computer games and seeing his friends. But he didn't like being stuck in a little cottage in the middle of the countryside, miles from anywhere, with nothing to do and nowhere to go.

7

It was their fourth day in the cottage. At nine o'clock in the morning, Harmony and Ben were sitting at the kitchen table, eating breakfast, when Jennifer came into the kitchen. She looked at her two eldest children and said, "We're going to have a family meeting. Here. In five minutes. Will you tell the others?" Barely waiting for the children to nod their agreement, she turned on her heel and marched out of the room.

Harmony and Ben looked at one another.

"What's going on?" said Ben.

"I don't know," said Harmony. "But it must be important. Mum looked really worried."

"Maybe something's happened to Dad."

"Or Jeremy."

"Or Granny."

"Maybe Grandpa's had another heart attack."

"If he had," said Ben, "do you think we'd have to go back to London?"

"You're sick," said Harmony. "I'm going to get Kitkat. You fetch Frank." She gulped down her final few mouthfuls of muesli, then hurried outside.

Of course Ben wouldn't have wanted his grandfather to have another heart attack. In fact, he could hardly imagine anything worse. But he couldn't help feeling cheerful at the prospect of leaving the cottage and going back home. He ran up the stairs, taking them two at a time, and went to the tiny bedroom at the back of the house.

He could see from the shape of the duvet on the bottom bunk that Frank was still in bed.

"Family meeting in five minutes," he said. "You'd better get up."

There was no response.

He spoke louder: "Frank?"

Nothing.

Ben clapped his hands. "Hey! Frank! Wakey-wakey!"

Still nothing.

Ben went to the head of the bed and pulled back the duvet. Frank was lying on his back, eyes closed, headphones clamped over his ears. Ben lifted one of the headphones and said, "Didn't you hear me? It's time to get up."

Without moving or even opening his eyes, Frank said, "No, thanks."

"You have to."

"Why?"

"There's a family meeting in five minutes."

Frank opened his eyes and sat up, removing the headphones from his ears and dropping them round his neck. "What's a family meeting?"

"It's when the whole family gets together and talks about something. Mum says it's our opportunity to express how we're really feeling. But it usually just means Mum wants to tell us something, so she needs us all in the same place at the same time."

"I'd rather stay in bed," said Frank.

"It's a family meeting," said Ben. "Everyone in the family has to come."

"I'm not a member of this family."

"Yes, you are."

"That's your opinion," said Frank. He replaced the headphones over his ears, settled back against his pillow and closed his eyes.

*

By the time that Ben got back to the kitchen, the others were already sitting around the kitchen table, waiting to start.

Jennifer said, "Where's Frank?"

"He's not coming," said Ben.

"Why not?"

"He said he's not coming to a family meeting because he's not a member of this family."

Without a word, Jennifer pushed back her chair and went upstairs. Five minutes later, she returned with Frank. "Sit down," she said.

Frank sat down.

Jennifer said, "Take off your headphones."

Frank took off his headphones.

"Thank you," said Jennifer. "As you know, my brother has allowed us to stay in this cottage on one condition. We have to look after his vegetable garden. We have to water his tomatoes and his beans. We have to stop the birds getting into his fruit cage. And, most importantly, we have to take care of his beloved strawberries. You all know this already, don't you?"

Harmony, Kitkat, Frank and Ben nodded. On their first day in the cottage, Jennifer had laid down a few ground rules. She had told them where they could go and where they couldn't. They could walk around the garden and through the woods near the cottage, but they weren't allowed to cross the road or climb any fences, because that would take them on to land which belonged to Hunchback Farm. The vegetable garden was also out of bounds. Uncle Barnaby would be furious if they damaged any of his valuable plants.

Especially his strawberries.

They all knew the story behind Uncle Barnaby's strawberries. A few years ago, he travelled through Tibet in the company of a llama, who he nicknamed Ethel. They ventured deep into unknown regions. Halfway up a mountain, hundreds of miles from the nearest hospital, Uncle Barnaby caught dysentery and would have died if he hadn't been nursed back to health by some monks. He stayed in their monastery for several months, befriending them and learning their ways. He even dabbled with the idea of becoming a monk himself, shaving his head and surrendering all attachment to material possessions. When he finally decided to come home, he left Ethel with the monks. In return, and as a memento of his stay, they gave him a strawberry plant. He carried it carefully back to England and planted it in his garden. Over the years, the strawberries had multiplied, and now they produced an annual crop unlike any other strawberries that you've ever tasted. They were tiny, succulent and exceptionally delicious. According to Uncle Barnaby, he and the head gardener at Kew Gardens were the only men in Europe who had their own crops of Tibetan strawberries. Once a year, they exchanged pots of jam.

"I went into the garden this morning," said Jennifer. "And I saw a shocking sight. Someone has done a dreadful thing. Some vandal, some hooligan, some stupid thug, has smashed that garden to pieces. They've pushed over the plants. They've trodden down the vegetables. And, worst of all, they've been tearing up the strawberries. Now, Barnaby said we could eat his strawberries. I could understand why someone might want to steal one or two of them. But why would anyone want to tear up the plants and trample them into the earth?" She looked at each of them in turn. "I can't imagine that any of you would be so stupid, so selfish or so horrible as to do anything like that. But I have to ask you. Harmony, Ben, Frank, Katherine – you weren't responsible for this, were you?"

One by one, they shook their heads.

Jennifer didn't quiz them. She trusted them to tell the truth. She just sighed. "When my brother said we could stay in this cottage, he made me promise we'd look after his garden. What's he going to say when he comes back from Peru and all his Tibetan strawberries have been killed?"

None of the children said a word. None of them knew what to say.

Jennifer ended the family meeting, as she always did, by asking if anyone had anything that they wanted to discuss. No one did. "Then I'd better get back to work," she said. "See you all later." She returned to her study.

Left to themselves, the four children didn't discuss what had just happened. Frank sloped upstairs. Kitkat grabbed her pink sunglasses, her big floppy hat and her copy of *Hello*, and went into the garden. Harmony turned to Ben and said, "What shall we have for supper – lasagne or goulash?"

"I don't mind," said Ben. "Whichever you like."

"We're going to have one or the other, so just choose. Which would you rather?"

"Lasagne, then."

"Good choice. Do you want to help me make it?"

"No."

"This is the twenty-first century, you know. We're not living in the middle ages. Men are supposed to do half the cooking."

"I don't mind cooking supper. Shall I do eggy bread?"

"Heart attacks all round," said Harmony. "No, thank you." She knelt by the fridge and pulled out the ingredients for lasagne.

Ben couldn't understand his sister. After four days of almost unbelievable boredom, something interesting had finally happened. And what did she do? Worry about what to have for supper.

He didn't care about lasagne or goulash. He had more important things to worry about. He was going to catch the strawberry thief.

Luckily, he knew exactly what to do.

8

ONE – ESTABLISH THE MOTIVE.

That was obvious. There could only be one motive for stealing strawberries. Someone wanted to eat them.

TWO – DRAW UP A LIST OF SUSPECTS.

Ben fetched a pen and a piece of paper. He wrote a list:

> *Jennifer*
> *Harmony*
> *Frank*
> *Ben*
> *Kitkat*
> *Neighbours*
> *Someone walking past*

Animals
Birds

Of those, he could immediately discount two. Kitkat didn't like strawberries, so she wouldn't have bothered stealing them. And he knew that he himself hadn't either. He drew lines through two names.

That left three people. Jennifer, Harmony and Frank. If his mother wanted the strawberries, she could just have taken them. Harmony wasn't the type of person who stole things. As for Frank. . . He wasn't so sure about Frank. He was a freak and a weirdo and a real pain to have around, but a thief? Maybe. Maybe not. It was impossible to know.

Ben crossed off two more names and put a question mark beside a third.

THREE – CHECK THE CRIME SCENE.

The vegetable garden was a rectangular plot of land with a fruit cage at one end and a compost heap at the other. Between the cage and the compost, there were six long beds. Four were filled with beans, peas, leeks, cabbages and tomatoes. The last two were devoted to strawberries.

The whole place had been smashed to pieces.

Someone had pulled up leeks and trampled down tomatoes. They had torn leaves from the cabbages and snatched beans from the beanpoles. Worst of all, they had plundered the strawberries, taking the fruit and tearing up the plants.

But who? And why? And how?

Ben paced slowly back and forth across the vegetable patch, examining the scene of the crime.

The fruit and veg were protected from predatory animals by a wooden gate, a tall fence and lots of barbed wire. Ben paced around every inch of the boundary, looking for gaps or holes, but the defences were completely secure. There was no way that deer, rabbits, badgers or any other animals could have got inside.

The strawberry plants themselves were covered with green netting, securely rooted into the soil by a series of pegs and poles. Anyone or anything who wanted to steal the strawberries would have to pull several wooden pegs out of the earth and push back the net. An eagle or a vulture might have been able to do that. But no eagles or vultures ever flew through Hunchback Valley. The thrushes, sparrows, wrens and other small birds which actually visited the vegetable garden couldn't possibly have pulled up those strong wooden pegs.

Ben went back to his list of suspects and added the information that he had deduced and discovered. His list now looked like this:

~~Jennifer~~
~~Harmony~~
Frank – ?
~~Ben~~
~~Kitkat~~
Neighbours
Someone walking past
~~Animals~~
~~Birds~~

That left three suspects: Frank, neighbours or someone walking past.

Frank. . . Yes, he was still a possibility.

Neighbours. . . There weren't any. The only other house in the valley was Hunchback Farm. Ben didn't know who lived there, but he couldn't imagine that farmers would bother stealing strawberries from someone else's vegetable garden. Wouldn't they have enough fruit of their own?

Someone walking past. . . No one walked past. Not a single person had come to Quarryman's Cottage since they'd arrived. A few cars occasionally drove along the road, but none ever came up the lane. Even the postman just left letters in a box by the gate. There were apparently public footpaths running through the valley, open to walkers, but Ben hadn't seen anyone using them.

Time for stage four.

FOUR – QUESTION THE WITNESSES.

Ben quizzed the others in turn. He asked where they had been yesterday and what they had been doing.

Jennifer had spent the entire day at her desk. She went into her study after breakfast and stayed there till supper. On the rare occasions that she lifted her eyes from the screen of her computer, she could see straight through the fence and into the vegetable garden, but she hadn't spotted any sign of an intruder.

Kitkat had spent most of yesterday sitting on the lawn, so she would have seen someone coming in or out of the gate.

Harmony had been pottering around the house and garden all day. She hadn't noticed anything suspicious.

Frank claimed to have spent the entire day

sitting on his bed, working on his computer, and said he hadn't even glanced out of the window.

If everyone was telling the truth, there were only two times that a thief could have taken the strawberries. At night or before breakfast. Ben couldn't believe that anyone could have sneaked into the vegetable garden during the hours of darkness without tripping over the fence, leaving footprints in the soil, or making enough noise to wake someone. Which left only one option. The thief must have arrived during the short space of daylight between dawn and breakfast.

FIVE – CATCH THE THIEF.

If we were at home, thought Ben, I could go to a shop and buy a webcam. I could set up a tripwire or build an alarm system or. . .

No, no, no, it wasn't even worth thinking about the wonderful gadgets which could have caught a crook red-handed, because the nearest shop selling them must have been a hundred miles away.

There was only one way to catch the thief.

He would have to do it himself.

When he went to bed, he set his alarm for 5.25 and put his phone under his pillow.

9

Ben sat up and stared at the thief.

He blinked. He couldn't believe what he was seeing. It looked like. . .

No, that would be impossible.

Maybe I'm dreaming, he thought.

But he knew he wasn't. You know when you're asleep. You don't have to pinch yourself to find out.

He was wide awake, sitting at the end of the garden, staring at the thief. And it was. . .

Really?

Was it?

He blinked again, trying to focus his still-sleepy eyes.

A small brown creature was crouching in the middle of the strawberry bed. Its tiny hands were moving quickly through the plants, gathering fruit.

It was bigger than a cat, but smaller than a dog. It was hunched over the ground like a person, but seemed to be covered with fur. It wasn't a deer, a fox, a rat or a rabbit. It looked like. . .

No, no, no, he told himself again. That wasn't possible. Not in the middle of the English countryside.

He pushed himself to his feet and took one step forward, then another. Although he was taking great care not to make any noise, his feet must have scuffed against the earth, because the thief whirled round, scattering handfuls of strawberries.

It would have been difficult to say which of them was more surprised. Neither of them moved. Nor did they make a sound. They just stayed very still and stared at one another.

The thief was a little brown monkey with black eyes and a long curly tail.

A monkey, thought Ben. A monkey? What's a monkey doing here? Where's it come from? Why's it stealing our strawberries? How did it. . . But before Ben could ask himself any more questions, the monkey whirled round and ran towards the fence.

Without even thinking, Ben ran after it.

The monkey moved surprisingly fast.

It sped across the vegetable patch on all fours, bounded through the beans, sprang across the tomatoes and hurled itself at the fence. With one great leap, the monkey swung straight over the top, avoiding all the barbed wire which had been layered there so carefully to prevent deer, badgers or rabbits from sneaking into the vegetable garden. And then it was gone, landing in a bed of long nettles on the other side of the fence, crashing through the undergrowth and heading for the road.

Ben followed as fast as he could. He hopped over beans and dodged round tomatoes, trying not to trample on any of his uncle's precious plants. And then he stopped. And stared at the fence. And wondered how he could get over the top without ripping his legs on those vicious-looking coils of barbed wire.

He couldn't. No way. The fence was too tall. The wire was too thick. And, unlike the monkey's, Ben's arms weren't strong enough to pull his own body weight into the air and fling himself, head over heels, over the top.

Time for Plan B.

Ben doubled back and sprinted across the vegetable beds, leaping over the tender young beans and dodging round the tomatoes, heading for the gate. He swung it open, charged out, and ran round the side of the vegetable garden.

He was just quick enough. Ahead of him, he could still see the monkey. It hadn't disappeared yet. The small brown creature was lolloping down the lane, heading for the gate and the main road. Then the road twisted and the monkey was gone, hidden behind the thick trees.

As Ben sprinted across the lawn, he told himself that this was the moment to stop. And turn round. And fetch help. He was never going to catch the monkey.

Even if he did – what then? What could he do with a monkey? Grab it? Trap it? Wrestle it to the ground? How? Don't monkeys have teeth? And claws? Much more sensible to run back to the house and call for help. Wake up Mum. Fetch a vet. Ring the RSPCA.

But what's so good about being sensible?

He reached the bend in the lane. Ahead, he couldn't see any sign of the thief, just trees and the empty road, but he kept running.

At the next bend, he saw the monkey, scrambling over the wooden gate that led to the road.

The monkey must have heard his footsteps, because it looked round and saw Ben. At that moment, the monkey could have jumped down the other side of the gate and escaped, but it chose not to. Instead, it stayed there, sitting on top of the gate, staring intently at Ben, as if it was fascinated by him or even wanted to communicate with him. Its long tail curled around the wooden bars of the fence, twitching as if it had a mind of its own.

Ben stopped running and stared back.

They watched one another.

Ben's eyes wandered over the monkey's face and body. Its fur was divided into two colours: dark brown on its arms, legs and back; white on its face, neck and belly. On the top of its head, it had a funny little clump of dark fur which looked like a quiff. Deep wrinkles ran across its forehead and round its eyes. If it had been a man, you'd have thought it was old and wise.

As Ben studied the monkey, he had the sense that the monkey was studying him in exactly the same way, noticing his distinctive markings, seeing how he was different to other members of his species, trying to gauge his thoughts, mood and character.

Ben had never been this close to a monkey before. In zoos, there are always ditches, walls and fences to protect you from the animals – and them from you. Seeing a monkey on telly is completely different to seeing one in the flesh. It's like the difference between watching an actor and meeting a real person.

There was another difference too. Something almost indefinable. Although this small, brown monkey looked very similar to the other monkeys that he'd seen in movies, documentaries and the zoo, the expression in its inquisitive little eyes made it look more intelligent – and more alive – than any other monkey that he'd ever seen before.

There were a few facts that Ben immediately understood about the monkey. He didn't know how he knew them; he just knew he knew them.

One: the monkey was a boy.

Two: the monkey wasn't scared.

Three: the monkey had things to tell him. Of course, the monkey couldn't speak. Monkeys can't. But if only Ben could find a way, there were all kinds of things that the monkey wanted to say, he was sure of that.

How could they communicate?

Should he say something? Or do something? And if so, what?

As far as Ben knew, the best way to make friends with an animal was always by offering it some food, but he didn't have any. And he didn't know anything about the sounds or gestures that monkeys make when they communicate with one another. So there was only one thing he could do. He'd have to speak English.

Feeling pretty stupid, but not knowing what else to do, Ben opened his mouth and said, "Hello, Mister Monkey."

In the silence, his voice sounded unusually loud, and Ben knew immediately that he'd made a mistake. Monkeys don't speak to one another. They communicate in other ways. Monkey ways. Waving their arms. Scratching their armpits. Showing off their bums. Not opening their mouths and saying, "Hello, Mister Monkey."

The monkey didn't say "hello" back again. Not in English. Or in Monkey. It just whirled round, scrambled along the fence and leaped into the nearest tree, trying to get away as fast as possible.

Ben ran towards the gate.

Using all five limbs – two legs and two arms and one long tail – the monkey swung itself into the branches.

Ben climbed the gate like a ladder, threw himself over the top and jumped down the other side. He landed badly, twisting his ankle.

"Ow!" he shouted.

He sprawled on the tarmac. A sharp twinge of pain ran up his right leg, but he ignored it and forced himself to stand up, ready to run.

He didn't know which way to go.

He looked up and down the road, but there was no sign of the monkey.

It could have gone anywhere. Up the road towards the village. Down the road towards the farm. Into a bed of nettles. Or it could just have swung through the trees, leaping from branch to branch, and disappeared into the woods.

That's the most likely, thought Ben. If I was a monkey, that's what I'd do. Up, up, up and away.

He stood there for a few minutes, peering into the trees, wondering where the monkey was hiding. He could have tried searching for it. His mother had encouraged him to go for a walk. He was allowed to wander through the woods as long as he kept to paths and didn't venture on to private land. But where would he start? Which way should he go?

He realized he didn't have a hope. The monkey would always see him first. While he trod on twigs and trampled down leaves, making masses of noise, the monkey would perch on a branch, high overhead, keeping quiet and looking down, having a good laugh at Ben's expense.

He waited for a few minutes longer, willing the monkey to come back again, hoping its curious nature might persuade it to take another peek at him, and then admitted to himself that it had gone.

"Bye, Mister Monkey," whispered Ben, his voice so quiet that even he could hardly hear himself. "Sorry if I scared you."

He tested his ankle, putting his full weight on his right leg. It didn't hurt so much now. Nothing was broken. Probably not even sprained. After breakfast, he'd be fine.

Breakfast, he thought. That sounds good.

He turned round, hauled himself carefully over the gate and, limping on his tender ankle, walked home.

10

When Ben got back to Quarryman's Cottage, Jennifer and Harmony were eating bowls of muesli at the kitchen table. They were surprised to see Ben not just up so early, but arriving through the garden rather than down the stairs from his bedroom. Jennifer said, "Hello, Benjy. Where have you been?"

"Out," said Ben.

"What have you been doing?"

"Nothing."

"Don't play games with me, Benjy. You never get up this early. What have you really been doing?"

For a moment, Ben was tempted to lie. He could have said that he'd been woken early by the birdsong and gone for a walk. The thief would have remained his own private property, his secret from the rest of the family. That might have been fun, but he couldn't resist telling them what had really happened. He said, "I found the strawberry thief."

Harmony sat up. "You caught him?"

"I didn't exactly catch him. But I saw him."

"Who is he?"

"I'll tell you," said Ben. "Just let me get some breakfast."

There was something very good about padding round the kitchen, fetching a bowl, a spoon and a packet of cereal, while his mother and his sister watched him, waiting for him to sit down and tell his story.

Ben let them wait. Taking his time, he poured himself a bowl of Shreddies, then described what he had seen and done. He began with his decision to set his alarm for dawn and ended with the monkey leaping off the wooden gate and disappearing down the road.

When he had finished, he sat back and folded his arms over his chest. "So, that's it," he said. "I've discovered who's been stealing the strawberries." He smiled.

For some reason, he couldn't imagine what, his mother and his sister didn't smile back.

Jennifer was watching him with narrowed eyes. She said, "What's going on, Benjy?"

"What do you mean?"

"Is there anything you want to tell me?"

"Like what?"

"I think you know."

"I don't."

Jennifer sighed. "You're not giving me much choice, Benjy, so I'll just ask you a straightforward question. Did you take the strawberries?"

"Me?"

"Well, did you?"

"No!"

"If you did, I don't mind. I just want you to tell the truth."

"I am telling the truth," said Ben. "I didn't take the strawberries. The monkey did."

"Oh, come on, Benjy. Do you really think monkeys are roaming round the English countryside, sneaking into other people's gardens and stealing their strawberries?"

Ben shrugged his shoulders. "I saw it."

"I know you've been bored, Benjy, but that's no reason to behave like this. You're only making things worse for yourself. Why don't you just tell me the truth? Did you or didn't you steal the strawberries?"

"I didn't," said Ben.

"Then who did?"

"I told you. It was the monkey."

"Stop being such a fool," said Jennifer in a brisk tone of voice, as if she'd finally lost patience with her stubborn son. "I can only think of two possible explanations for what you've just told me. Either you've invented this silly story because you're bored. Or you're the one who's been taking the strawberries. Which is it, Benjy?"

There is a third possible explanation, Ben could have said. And that is: I'm telling the truth. Instead, he just sighed and said, "I guess I was bored."

"You didn't take the strawberries?"

"No, Mum."

"If you did, I don't mind."

"I didn't," said Ben. "And I'm sorry I told you about the monkey."

Jennifer looked at her son, staring into his eyes, trying to decide whether to believe him. Finally, she pushed back her chair and stood up. "We'll talk about this again tonight. See you later, darlings. You don't mind clearing up breakfast, do you?" Without waiting for an answer, she took her coffee into her study and closed the door.

Harmony put the milk in the fridge, then carried the bowls to the sink and washed up.

Ben didn't offer to help. He was staring at his

hands, lost in thought. He could understand why his mum might question the existence of the monkey, but this was different. Didn't she know him? Did she really think he was a thief – and a liar?

11

When Harmony finished the washing-up, she dried her hands on a towel and looked at Ben. She said, "Are you OK?"

"Yes."

"Sure?"

"I'm fine."

Harmony folded the towel and hung it over the back of a chair. "I'm going to walk to the shop in the village. We need some bread and milk. Do you want to come with me?"

"Not really."

"Come on, Ben. It'll be fun. Better than sitting here all day, feeling cross with Mum."

Ben looked at his sister. "Do you believe me?"

"I don't think you stole the strawberries, Benjy. You're not a thief."

"What about the monkey? Do you believe that?"

"I don't know."

"So you think I was lying?"

"No. You're not a liar."

"Then why don't you believe me?"

"I do believe you," said Harmony. "I believe you believe it, anyway."

"What's that supposed to mean?"

"I'm sure you thought you saw a monkey. I'm just not so sure you actually did. Our brains are funny machines, Ben. I get things slightly wrong all the time. We all do. I think I've seen something or someone's said something and actually I've seen or heard something completely different."

"Do you think I'm an idiot? I know what a monkey looks like."

"There's no need to snap at me," said Harmony. "I'm just saying you might have imagined it. Maybe you saw a rabbit or a pigeon or some strange shadow and you thought it was a monkey. Things like that happen all the time."

"I know the difference between a rabbit and a monkey."

"There is another possibility," said Harmony. "Maybe you dreamt it."

"I wasn't dreaming," said Ben.

"Some dreams feel very real."

"I'm not a moron. I can tell the difference between dreams and reality."

"You did say you'd fallen asleep."

"Yeah, I fell asleep. And then I woke up. And then I saw the monkey." Ben shook his head. "I've already told you exactly what happened. Why don't you believe me?"

"I do," said Harmony. "I just think you might be a bit confused."

"Whatever," said Ben. He pushed his chair back and stood up. "See you later." He headed for the door.

Harmony called after him: "Are you sulking? Ben? Benjy? I hope you're not going to slam the—"

BANG!

Ben grinned. He could hear Harmony shouting at him from the kitchen, but he took no notice. He'd had enough of her and Mum and all the rest of them.

He headed down the hallway towards the front door.

It's so unfair, he thought. I didn't steal any strawberries. I'm the only one who knows who did. And so what happens? They think I'm a liar and a thief.

Oh, it was all his own stupid fault. He shouldn't

have told them. He should have followed his instincts and kept the monkey to himself.

From now on, thought Ben, I won't tell the others anything. The monkey will be my secret. Till I actually find it and bring it back here. Then they'll have to believe me.

12

News travelled fast.

Around midday, Ben was sitting in the garden, thinking through the events of that morning, when Kitkat sauntered across the grass and stopped opposite him. She said, "I hear you met a monkey."

"Who told you that?"

"A little birdie."

"You mean Harmony?"

"This little birdie might have been called Harmony, yes. Or she might not. But she made me promise not to tell you what she'd told me."

"Then why are you telling me?"

"Because I want to know all about it," said Kitkat. She threw herself on the grass and stared up at Ben expectantly, her eyes gleaming. "I looooove monkeys. I want to know every detail. Where did you see him? And when? Don't leave anything out. I want to know *exactly* what happened. Start at the very beginning and tell me absolutely everything."

"There's nothing to tell."

"That's not what the little birdie said. The little birdie said you'd gone searching for the strawberry thief and you'd caught a monkey."

"Maybe the little birdie doesn't know what she's talking about."

"Oh, just tell me what happened. What kind of monkey did you see? Big? Small? Brown? Black? Where was it? What did it do? Tell me everything!"

"Like I said, there's nothing to tell. The whole thing was just a dream."

"A dream?" Kitkat blinked. "What do you mean, a dream?"

"I dreamt I saw a monkey."

"You were asleep? That sort of dream?"

"Yes."

"Oh," said Kitkat. "And what happened?"

"I dreamt I went into the vegetable garden and saw a monkey stealing the strawberries."

"That's it?"

"Yes."

"Doesn't sound very exciting."

"It wasn't," said Ben. "It was just an ordinary dream about a dumb monkey."

Kitkat sighed. "I thought things were finally going to get interesting round here. Silly me."

13

The second morning was much more difficult than the first.

At 5.25, when Ben slid his hand under the pillow and switched off his alarm, he almost went back to sleep. He was tired. He would have given just about anything to lie down and close his eyes. But he forced himself to roll out of bed.

He climbed down from his bunk and grabbed his clothes. As he was heading towards the door, a voice cut through the silence.

"What are you doing?"

On the lower bunk, Frank was sitting up in bed, staring at him.

Ben put his finger to his lips. "Shhhh. Don't wake the others."

This time, Frank whispered. "What are you doing?"

"Nothing."

"Doesn't look like nothing."

"I can't sleep," hissed Ben. "I'm going for a walk."

"Why did you set your alarm so early?"

"I didn't."

"You're a terrible liar."

"I'm not lying."

"Liar."

"Believe what you like," whispered Ben. "I don't care." He walked out of the room, slid the door silently shut after him and tiptoed along the corridor. He hadn't looked back once, but he was sure Frank had watched him every step of the way.

He'd better not follow me, thought Ben. He'd better keep his nose out of my affairs.

Downstairs, Ben pulled on his clothes and laced up his shoes. He stood in the hallway for a few seconds, listening for noises, but the house was quiet. Frank must have gone back to sleep. His sisters and his mum hadn't heard a thing. He was safe.

He went into the kitchen and opened the fridge. If he was going to make friends with the monkey, he should take some food. But what did monkeys eat? He peered at the shelves. Salami? Yoghurt? Carrots? Cheddar cheese? None of them sounded very monkey-ish.

There was one thing that Ben knew the monkey liked. Strawberries. But there weren't any in the house. He could have stolen some from Uncle Barnaby's vegetable patch, but then he really would be a strawberry thief.

In movies, monkeys ate bananas. Ben knew it was a mistake to mix up movies with real life, but he decided to take a chance. He closed the fridge. There were eight bananas in the fruit bowl. He grabbed the whole bunch and hurried outside.

It was another cool, clear morning. The sun hadn't yet appeared in the sky, but its first gleams were just visible on the tops of the trees. Ben walked round the house, unlatched the gate and tiptoed into the vegetable patch. He'd been hoping the monkey might be there already, snatching a few early strawberries, but the beds were empty.

Ben sat on the same patch of grass as the day before and settled down to wait. He kept the bananas close. When the monkey arrived, he'd use them like a peace offering. Today he wouldn't scare the monkey away. On their second meeting, they were going to become friends.

When he arrives, thought Ben, I'll offer him some bananas. And then we'll talk. I won't say anything dumb like, "Hello, Mister Monkey." I'll communicate with him in a more monkey-ish fashion. I might scratch my armpits. And waggle my bum. He'll want to be friends with me. He'll think I'm some kind of monkey. An unusually big monkey without a tail or any fur on my face.

If he arrives.

As the morning wore on, Ben began to worry that the monkey wasn't coming. The sun rose over the trees. The air grew warmer. A robin and a couple of blackbirds darted among the vegetables, picking worms from the soil, and some crows flew overhead, but there was no sign of a monkey.

Ben felt hungry. He counted the bananas. There were eight. The monkey could surely spare one.

He ate a banana. It was so delicious, he couldn't resist eating another. He'd have liked a third, but he stopped himself. Enough was enough. He put the remaining six bananas on the grass, folded his arms and waited.

14

"What are you doing here?"

Ben sat up, blinking.

His mother was standing over him, holding a bright blue colander. "If you want to go camping, Benjy, we do have a tent."

Ben looked around. The sun was shining brightly on the vegetable patch. Hours must have passed since he'd got up.

I'm an idiot, he thought. I've done it again.

He pushed himself to his feet and brushed the dirt from his jeans. "What time is it?"

"Breakfast time." His mother held up the colander. "That's why I've come to pick some redcurrants. What are you doing here?"

"I wanted some fresh air."

"Why didn't you just open your window?"

"I didn't want to wake Frank."

"Hmmm. OK." Jennifer frowned. She didn't look convinced.

To cut off any more of her questions, Ben said, "Do you want a hand picking redcurrants? It's much quicker with two people."

"That's very nice of you, Benjy. I'd like to get enough for everyone. Let's start at this end." Jennifer pointed to the top of the fruit cage. "There are still lots left up there."

As the two of them walked along the narrow, grassy path that marked the boundary of the strawberry patch, Ben remembered something. He looked back at the patch of flattened grass where he had just been sitting.

A couple of banana skins were lying on the ground, exactly where his feet had been, but there was no sign of any more.

He'd only eaten two from the bunch. Where were the others?

He looked around, wondering if he could have pushed them away in his sleep, but he couldn't see them. So where were they? What had happened to the last six bananas?

His mother said, "Have you lost something?"

"No."

"Then what are you looking for?"

"Nothing."

Jennifer folded her arms and glared at her son. "You may think I'm a complete idiot," she said. "But I can see you're looking for something. Why don't you tell me what it is?"

"Just these," said Ben. He hurried back to where he had been sitting and grabbed the two banana skins. "I want to put them on the compost."

"Oh, Benjy." Jennifer smiled affectionately at her son. "Did you bring them for 'the monkey'?"

"No, Mum. You were right. There's never been a monkey. It was just a stupid dream." He tossed the two banana skins on to the compost. "Are we going to pick redcurrants or what?"

"Let's get picking," said Jennifer. She unlatched the door of the fruit cage. Ben followed her inside. They knelt beside the redcurrant bushes. Jennifer placed the colander on the ground between them and said, "You start there. I'll start here. We'll meet in the middle. OK?"

"Sure," said Ben. He knelt on the ground, picked a handful of redcurrants and dropped them in the colander.

They worked in silence for a couple of minutes. Then Jennifer smiled at her son and said, "We all like telling stories, don't we?"

"I guess," said Ben, not entirely sure what his mother was talking about.

"Of course we do. It's part of being human. I want you to be inventive and creative. Do you understand?"

"Yes, Mum," said Ben.

"But there's a difference between telling stories and telling lies. I never, ever want you to lie to me. You wouldn't, would you?"

"No, Mum."

"Good. So let's not hear any more about monkeys. OK?"

"OK," said Ben. As he reached for a hanging bundle of redcurrants, he saw a splash of yellow. For a moment, he couldn't understand where or what it was. Then his eyes adjusted their focus and he realized he could see a banana skin, hanging from one of the lower branches of a large tree at the back of the vegetable garden.

"What are you looking at?" said Jennifer.

"Nothing."

Jennifer turned to see what Ben had been staring at. From where she was sitting, the banana skin was hidden. She turned back to Ben. "I don't want to be difficult about this," she said. "I'd like us to be friends, Benjy. But friends don't lie to one another.

Friends always tell the truth. You understand that, don't you?"

"Yes, Mum."

"I know you've been bored, Benjy. I know you don't really want to be here. And I know you're not happy about sharing your room with Frank. I'm very sorry about all that. But I can't help you if you don't talk to me. You've got to be honest with me, Benjy. Why don't you tell me what's going on?"

"There's nothing going on."

Jennifer sighed. "Is it my fault? Am I a bad mother?"

"No, Mum."

"Really, darling?"

"Yes, Mum."

"I do try my best."

"I know you do, Mum."

"Thank you for saying that, Benjy. I have to admit, it's not easy. With your father as he is. And your stepfather as *he* is. And all you children." She sighed again and picked up the colander. "Let's go inside and have some lovely breakfast."

"I'm coming in a minute," said Ben. "I just want to stay here for a bit."

"Why?"

"I like the fresh air."

Jennifer stared at her son for a moment, then sighed. "Do whatever you like," she said. She let herself out of the fruit cage and strolled to the house, carrying the redcurrants.

When his mother had gone, Ben peered into the tall trees. He hoped he might notice some shivering leaves and catch sight of a small brown monkey, leaping from branch to branch, but there was nothing to be seen except a single banana skin, swinging gently in the breeze.

If there's one banana, thought Ben, there must be more.

He started walking down the lane, staring at the trees, searching for further evidence of the monkey's presence. Halfway down the lane – yes! there! – he found another banana skin, dumped on the grass. He picked it up and walked slowly towards the road, turning his head from left to right, staring at the trees and bushes, searching for any sign of the final four bananas.

He reached the gate without seeing a single one. Maybe the monkey had gone a different way. Right now, he was probably lying on a sunlit patch of grass, his paws clasped around his belly, sleeping off his enormous breakfast.

The thought of breakfast made Ben feel hungry,

but he wasn't ready to give up yet. He clambered over the gate and jumped down into the road. This time, he was careful to bend his legs before he landed, protecting his ankles.

He looked up and down the road. The tarmac was empty. No monkeys to be seen. No bananas either.

He wondered which way the monkey had gone. Up to the village? Down to the farm? Or into the woods? There was no way of knowing. Whichever way he'd gone, he had disappeared, leaving no trace.

Breakfast, thought Ben. I'm going to have a big breakfast. Cereal and toast and maybe a boiled egg too. Then I'll come back here and search properly.

As he turned round, heading home, he glimpsed a flash of yellow. What was that? Where was it? He looked up.

There was a single banana skin flopped on the top of the high brick wall.

Ben could imagine exactly what had happened. The monkey must have swung through the trees, run along to the end of that spindly branch and leaped through the air, landing on the wall.

If I was a monkey, thought Ben, that's what I'd do too. It was the perfect place for breakfast. Safe and secure. No chance of being caught. You'd get a good view in every direction and see anyone long before they reached you.

And then, when the monkey had finished his breakfast, he'd dumped the banana skin where he'd been sitting, scrambled down the other side of the wall and gone into the quarry.

Well, that was that. Ben couldn't follow the monkey any further. The wall was more than twice his height. Three times, maybe. Without a ladder, he'd never be able to get over the top.

A ladder, thought Ben. I know where I've seen a ladder.

He turned and hurried back to the house.

15

All kinds of junk had been stuffed haphazardly into the dusty wooden shed. Ben could see spades, rakes, trowels, flowerpots, paintbrushes, buckets, candlesticks, suitcases, saucepans, jam jars, coils of wire, parasols, some cricket stumps, a croquet set, a model yacht with a broken mast, a top hat, a bicycle wheel, a pink plastic flamingo, an antique radio, empty beer bottles, cracked mirrors, rusty scissors and, buried at the back, behind piles of plastic bags and cardboard boxes, an old metal ladder.

Another time, thought Ben, I should come back here and explore. Some of this stuff looks fun. But not now. He started clearing a path between the ladder and the door.

Half an hour later, Ben was breathless, exhausted, covered in cobwebs and standing outside the shed, staring at the ladder, wondering what to do next.

He'd managed to drag it through the door and on to the grass, but couldn't move it any further. The ladder was twice his height and impossibly heavy. He'd have to ask someone to help.

He didn't want to. The monkey was his secret. He'd already discovered the dangers of telling the truth to his family. But he had no choice.

He thought through his options.

Not Mum, obviously.

Frank would be best. He was older than Ben and stronger. He could probably carry the ladder on his own. But he was a freak. Ben didn't want to have to talk to him, let alone ask him for help.

Harmony was practical and sensible and full of good ideas, but she'd ask too many awkward questions. Before agreeing to carry the ladder, she'd insist on knowing why Ben wanted it. As soon as he told her, she'd refuse to help. *You're not allowed to climb over the wall*, she'd say. *That's private property. Can't you read the signs?*

Which left only one person.

Kitkat was sitting on the grass, reading a book. When Ben sat beside her, she said "Hiya" without even looking up.

"Hi," said Ben. He sat there for a moment,

searching for the right words to use, then said, "You remember my dream?"

"No."

"The one about the monkey."

"Hmmm," murmured Kitkat, still not lifting her head from her book.

"It wasn't a dream."

"What do you mean?"

"I didn't *dream* about a monkey stealing the strawberries. I *saw* a monkey stealing the strawberries."

That made her look up. She said, "What kind of monkey?"

Ben told her what had happened, describing how and when he had seen the monkey, and what it looked like.

Kitkat listened, fascinated, and managed not to ask too many questions, although she couldn't resist trying to guess where the monkey had come from. "Maybe he escaped from a circus."

"Don't think so," said Ben. "If there was a circus near here, we'd have seen it."

"A zoo, then."

"There aren't any zoos either."

"He must belong to a pop star," said Kitkat. "No, a princess. She keeps him as a pet. She must be missing him. I bet she's offering a huge reward."

She sat up. "It's all so exciting! What are we going to do next? How are we going to find him?"

Ben described his plan.

"That's a good plan," said Kitkat. "I'll put my shoes on. Shall we take a picnic?"

"You're not coming with me. You're just going to help me carry the ladder."

"Why can't I come too?"

"Because I'm going alone."

"Why?"

"Because it's my monkey. Finders keepers."

"You don't *own* it," said Kitkat. "You just happen to have been the first person to see it. How can you say it's *yours*?"

"If I find it, I'll bring it back. Then you can play with it too. I'll share, I promise, if you can just help me with this one small thing."

"I know what we should do," said Kitkat with a mischievous smile. "We should tell Harmony."

"You can tell her what you like. She won't believe you."

"I bet she will. When she hears we're going to climb over the wall, she'll want to come too. It'll be much more fun with three of us." Kitkat stood up and trotted towards the house.

Ben ran after her and blocked her path. "Don't."

"Why not?" said Kitkat, her face a picture of innocence.

"You know what she's like. She's such a goody-goody. She'll probably ring the police and report a missing monkey. Or tell Mum. And she definitely wouldn't let us climb over the wall. Anyway, we don't need her. I can find him on my own. I just need some help carrying the ladder."

"I still think we should tell her," said Kitkat.

"Also, if there is a reward, she wouldn't want it. She'd give it back. You know what she'd say." Ben imitated Harmony's voice: "*We have enough money, thank you very much. You keep the reward. Doing the right thing is enough for us.*"

Kitkat thought about this for a moment, then nodded. Ben was right. Harmony believed you should do good things simply because you were a good person, not for any reward.

"We won't tell her," said Kitkat. "On one condition."

"And that is?"

"We split the reward. Half-half."

"Done," said Ben. If he'd thought there was going to be a reward, he would have negotiated better terms, but he didn't. He offered his hand.

They shook on the deal.

16

Ben foraged through the fridge and the cupboards, searching for snacks. Not for himself. For the monkey. To make friends.

The way to a monkey's heart is through his stomach.

In the fruit bowl, there were two apples, three plums and a handful of cherries. He took the lot. If Harmony happened to notice all the fruit was missing, he'd say he needed the vitamins.

He grabbed a packet of cashew nuts from the cupboard. Didn't monkeys like nuts? He thought they did. He put the fruit and the nuts in a small red backpack, slung it over his shoulders and went to find Kitkat.

Together, they walked round the house to the shed, then half-dragged, half-carried the ladder through the garden and down the lane. It was unbelievably heavy. Their arms ached and their fingers went numb. Whenever the pain became unbearable, they paused for a quick rest, putting the ladder on the ground and shaking their arms, but Ben wouldn't let Kitkat stop for more than a few seconds.

Ben had prepared a story in case anyone saw them – he had seen a kite stuck in a tree, he'd say, and wanted to get it down – but didn't need to use it. As far as he could tell, they hadn't been noticed.

At the end of the lane, Ben opened the gate. He and Kitkat carried the ladder across the road, then propped it against the wall. A white sign was nailed into the bricks. Ben read the words to himself.

PRIVATE PROPERTY – KEEP OUT
GUARD DOGS PATROL THESE PREMISES

He tore his eyes away. The sign probably wasn't telling the truth. The owners of the quarry must just be hoping to scare trespassers away. They couldn't really have any guard dogs. He'd have heard them barking in the middle of the night.

The ladder's highest rung almost reached the top of the wall.

"You have to hold it here and here," said Ben, placing Kitkat's hands on the ladder. "Hold tight.

ut don't let go. Your job is to stop it sliding around while I'm climbing."

"I know," said Kitkat. She leaned against the base of the ladder, using her weight to wedge it against the wall.

Ben shook the ladder. It seemed secure. He put his foot on the first rung.

"Don't fall off," said Kitkat.

"I won't," said Ben, trying to sound more confident than he felt. He climbed slowly. With every step, the ladder wobbled more.

He reached the top of the wall and peered over the other side.

Directly below him, a deep bank of nettles ran in both directions along the length of the wall. To his left, there was an impenetrable forest. The quarry was on his right. From his vantage point, he couldn't see more than the edges of the carved-out hillsides and a few dark entrances which probably led into mines and caves, but it looked like just the sort of place that a monkey might hide.

He pushed himself off the top of the ladder, swung his right leg over and sat astride the wall as if he were riding a horse.

The ground was a long way down. Even worse, he would have to jump right into the middle of the nettles. He had no way of knowing what lay under them. There could be a pit, a ditch, a stream or even a series of metal traps with sharp teeth, primed to clamp around an intruder's leg.

He should have brought a rope. He could have lowered himself slowly down into the nettles, testing the ground with his feet before risking his whole weight. But he didn't want to go back now. There was only one way to get down. He'd have to jump.

He looked back at Kitkat. She was standing on the ground, still holding the bottom of the ladder. Seen from the top of the wall, her round face, staring up at him, looked tiny.

Ben knew no one would notice his absence till supper time. Even so, he said, "Don't tell anyone where I've gone. Even if they ask."

"I won't, I promise," said Kitkat. "But you will be careful, won't you?"

"Of course I will."

"How are you going to get out again?"

"I'll find a way."

"But how?"

"I don't know. There must be an entrance somewhere. A gate or a door. I'll be fine."

"What shall I do if you don't come back?"

"Don't be silly," said Ben. "Of course I'll come back."

"But what if you don't? You might get lost. Or eaten by guard dogs. What shall I do then?"

"I'm going to be fine," said Ben, not even wanting to imagine all the things that could possibly go wrong. "You won't tell Mum?"

"I won't tell anyone."

"Or Harmony?"

"I just said I won't tell anyone."

"You promise?"

"Cross my heart, hope to die, stick a needle in my eye."

"Good. See you later."

Ben swung his other leg over the wall. Now he was sitting on the top, both feet dangling down towards the ground.

Time to jump, he thought. Jump! But he hesitated. Why? What was stopping him? The thought of the nettles? The mystery of what might lie under them? Or just the fear of falling?

At school, in swimming, Ben once had to plunge off the high diving board. He didn't want to. But there was only one thing worse than jumping and that was retreating down the ladder, watched by everyone in his class. So he closed his eyes, took a deep breath and threw himself into the air. His stomach smarted for hours afterwards, but hitting the water hadn't killed him, and he'd learnt a good lesson. If you're going to do something scary, do it fast, before you have time to think too much. Thinking just makes you even more scared.

He slid forward and dropped towards the ground.

17

"Ben?"

He heard a small, quiet voice. The voice of a girl. She sounded a long way away.

"Hey, Ben?"

He was lying on his side. His arm hurt. Before he remembered where he was or how he might have got there, he heard the voice again. It seemed to be coming from directly above him.

"Ben? Are you OK?"

It was Kitkat's voice.

"I'm fine," said Ben.

"You don't look fine."

"How do you know? You can't see me."

"Yes, I can."

Ben looked up. The brick wall towered above him. At the top, silhouetted against the sun, he could see Kitkat's face, peering down at him. He said, "What are you doing?"

"I was worried. You were quiet for such a long time. I kept shouting, but you didn't answer."

"I'm fine now," said Ben. When he hit the ground, he must have fallen badly. Maybe he hit his head and blacked out. He rubbed his scalp. Ow! Yup. Right there.

He hoisted himself to his feet and tested his weight on his legs. Everything worked. His ankles would probably ache for a day or two, but nothing had been broken. The worst thing was the nettle stings. His hands, ankles, neck and face were covered in them and they were starting to itch. He tipped his head back, looked at Kitkat and said, "You shouldn't be climbing the ladder. There's no one holding the base."

"Don't worry," said Kitkat. "I'm not going to fall off."

"It's your funeral," said Ben. He took a couple of steps away from the wall, pushing through the nettles, ignoring the few tough ones that managed to sting him through his jeans. "See you later."

"I'm coming with you," said Kitkat.

"No way," said Ben. "Baby sisters not allowed. Climb down the ladder and go home. Hey! What are you doing? Kitkat! Stop it! Go back down again! You're not allowed to do that!"

Kitkat sat astride the wall, taking no notice of her brother, then leaned back the way that she had come. There was the sound of metal scraping against brick, then a crash.

Ben knew what that crash meant. She had pushed the ladder over. Stranding herself on top of the wall.

"That was stupid," he said. "Now what are you going to do?"

"Jump."

"Don't be an idiot. You can't jump from there."

"Why not?"

"It's too high. You'll kill yourself."

"Not if you catch me."

"Don't be crazy. You're much too heavy."

"You'll have to," said Kitkat, swinging her other leg over the wall and perching on the edge, looking as comfortable as if she were sitting on an ordinary chair. "Here I come!"

"No," said Ben. "Wait!"

His little sister took no notice. She threw herself straight at him.

Ben had only two options. He could try to catch her. Or he could dodge out of the way. If he dodged, she'd smash straight into the ground. He stood where he was and put his arms in the air.

Kitkat was a small girl. Like most small girls, she didn't weigh much. But like any other small girl who drops three metres through the air, she gained a lot of momentum between the top and the bottom. When she landed in Ben's arms, she knocked him to the ground.

He sprawled backwards into the nettles. His head smacked against the grass. For the second time that day, the world went dark.

The next thing he heard was a voice.

"Ben? Ben? Are you OK?"

"I'm alive," said Ben. "At least I think I am." He sat up, stretched his limbs and checked for damage. He was covered with lumps, bumps, bruises, stings and rashes, but there didn't seem to be any blood and nothing was broken.

Kitkat said, "Are you sure you're OK?"

"I'd be a lot better without you."

Kitkat ignored his last comment and sprang to her feet. "This is so totally cool," she said, a big smile on her face. "Let's start exploring. Come on, get up. What are you waiting for?"

"You can explore as much as you like," said Ben. "I'm going to find the monkey."

"I'll come with you."

"No, you won't. I told you before, baby sisters aren't invited. I'm doing this alone."

Kitkat stared at her brother with wide, surprised eyes. "What am I going to do?"

"You should have thought about that before throwing yourself off the wall."

"But—"

"Why don't you stay here? Sit down. Keep quiet. When I've found the monkey, I'll come back and get you."

"I can't stay here on my own. I'm only seven!"

Ben looked at Kitkat and shook his head. I'm older than her, he thought. Probably more intelligent. Definitely more sensible. Why does she never listen to a word I say?

He sighed. What was he supposed to do with her now? Once she'd jumped off the top of the wall, there was no way to get her up again. And she was right. He couldn't leave her here on her own. If anything happened, everyone would blame him. He'd even blame himself. Big brothers have to look after their little sisters. That's just the way the world works.

"Come on, then," he said. "But you'd better behave."

"I always behave," said Kitkat. "Sometimes I

behave well and sometimes I behave badly." She giggled and then, seeing Ben wasn't amused, wiped the smile from her face. "I'll be good."

"You'd better. And when we get back, I don't want you blabbing about what we've done. You've got to promise not to tell anyone what's happened."

"I promise I won't tell anyone," said Kitkat. "Cross my heart, hope to die, stick a needle in my eye."

"Only a moron would trust your promises," said Ben. "I guess that makes me a moron. Come on, let's go. You'd better keep up. I'm not going to wait for you."

He plunged through the nettles and headed towards the quarry.

He was pretty sure that Kitkat wouldn't follow him. She wouldn't want to risk the nettles. She was smaller than him and wearing a skirt rather than trousers. Her legs would be savaged.

But she didn't even hesitate. She stomped straight through the thick barricade of waist-high nettles, staying just behind her brother.

When they emerged from the nettlebed, Ben noticed that his sister's legs were covered with a scarlet wallpaper of rashes, stings and scratches. Her skirt had hardly protected her. She'd itch for hours. But she hadn't uttered a single word of complaint.

Kitkat was annoying, he thought. Selfish too. And he'd much rather have been alone. But at least she hadn't complained about the nettles. She wasn't so bad after all.

He didn't say anything to her. He didn't want her to get a big head. But he slowed down, walking at her pace rather than his, and told her what he was planning to do. "We'll look round the quarry," he said. "Maybe someone's living there. A tramp. Someone from a circus. Whoever. The monkey might belong to them. But don't make any noise, OK? I don't want them to hear us before we see them."

"I'll be very quiet," whispered Kitkat. "I promise."

"Good. Come on, then."

When they reached the quarry, Ben saw a bright yellow banana skin lying on the gravel.

He picked it up and looked around, staring at the hills and the caves, the trees and the thistles, the rocks and the boulders, wondering how a small, brown monkey could have found himself in a deserted, disused quarry, miles from anywhere.

Who or what could have brought him here? And where was he now?

Once, hundreds of men must have worked in this quarry, cutting heavy lumps of stone and loading them on to carts. Now, nothing was left except a misshapen hillside covered with scars and holes. Massive boulders and half-demolished buildings littered the quarry's floor. Round the sides, dark entrances led into the caves.

A gravel track led out of the quarry and disappeared into the woods. Years ago, this might have been a well-kept road, but the surface was now overgrown, cracked and covered with potholes.

Ben quickly counted the caves. He could see twenty-three. He was just deciding which one to search first when Kitkat lifted her arm and pointed. "Look," she whispered. "Look!"

Ben turned to see what she was pointing at.

On the other side of the quarry, two creatures had emerged from one of the caves. At first glance, Ben thought they might be people. But no humans had such hunched shoulders or such long arms or such thick, black fur covering their bodies.

Kitkat was so excited that she forgot to whisper and said in a loud clear voice, "They're real live monkeys!"

"Sshhh," hissed Ben, but it was too late. The monkeys had already heard her. First one lifted its head and turned to see where the noise had come from. Then the other did too. For a second, they glared at the children, and then, moving in perfect unison, as if a signal had passed between them, they scampered in the opposite direction, running on all fours.

Kitkat ran after them.

After a few paces, she realized Ben wasn't following her. "What are you waiting for?" she shouted.

"We're meant to be finding my monkey," said Ben. "We should be searching the caves."

"What do you mean, 'your monkey'? Isn't that him?"

"No, no, he looked completely different."

Kitkat turned and looked at the monkeys. They had reached the edge of the quarry and were now disappearing into the trees. She turned back, her face full of regret, and said, "The caves will still be there later. But those monkeys won't. And I bet you, if we find them, we'll find yours too."

She was probably right, thought Ben. And if they didn't manage to catch these two monkeys, they could always retrace their steps and search the caves later.

"Let's go," he said.

They sprinted across the quarry, skidding on gravel and stumbling over loose rocks, and plunged into the forest.

18

They had only been walking for a couple of minutes when Ben realized they were lost.

The monkeys had vanished. Trees surrounded them. In every direction, the forest looked the same – a jumble of leaves and branches.

Ben wasn't sure which way they should be heading or where they had come from, but he didn't want to turn round now. They had to keep going till they found the monkeys.

A strange noise echoed through the air. It sounded something like a bark or a roar. It wasn't loud, but it was deep, and the reverberations lasted for a long time.

Kitkat stopped and turned to Ben. "What was that?"

"I don't know," said Ben, trying to sound calmer than he felt. "The guard dogs, maybe. Do you remember those signs on the wall?"

"Oh, yes," said Kitkat. "I'd forgotten about the dogs." She gave Ben a small, nervous smile, and kept walking.

Guard dogs, thought Ben.

He had tried to sound reassuring, not wanting to scare Kitkat, but the thought of guard dogs made him exceedingly nervous.

If a pack of Alsatians charged towards him, froth dripping from their jaws, what would he do? Run? No, that would be pointless. He couldn't possibly run faster than dogs. Hide? There was nowhere to hide. Climb a tree? Only one problem. He didn't know how to. City boys like Ben can't climb trees. If he couldn't run, hide or climb a tree, he'd just have to lie on the ground, play dead and hope the dogs didn't bite too hard.

He stared into the woods, wondering what was lurking there, staring back at him.

The sound came again, louder this time and clearer too. It sounded more like a deep-throated roar than a bark.

Kitkat turned round. "That's not a dog," she said.

"It must be the monkeys, then."

"Monkeys don't roar. It sounded more like. . . It sounded like a lion."

"You don't get lions in the middle of the English countryside."

"You don't get monkeys either," said Kitkat.

As Ben was trying to think of an answer to that, the noise echoed through the woods a third time, even louder than before. Whatever it was, the beast was coming closer.

Kitkat's face had lost all its colour and her eyes were darting from side to side, searching the woods. In a small, frightened voice, she said, "Do you think we should turn back?"

"There's not much point," said Ben, trying to sound calm. "We can't get over the wall without a ladder."

"Maybe we should get ready to defend ourselves."

"How?"

"We could make a weapon."

"With what?"

"I don't know, I don't know, I don't know. But we've got to do *something*. I don't want to be eaten by a lion."

"Don't worry, Kitkat. There is absolutely no way that you're going to get eaten by a lion."

"How do you know?"

"If a lion comes anywhere near us, I'll throw

myself in front of him. While he's eating me, you'll have time to escape."

Kitkat giggled. "Would you really do that?"

"Of course I would," said Ben. "What do you think brothers are for?"

Kitkat giggled again, louder. "I had always wondered."

"Now you know. We're lion food. That's the point of us." Ben took a couple of paces forward, then looked back at his little sister. "Tell you what, Kitkat. Seeing a lion would be quite interesting. And I wouldn't mind getting another look at those black monkeys. But what I really want to do is catch my monkey, the one who stole the strawberries. I'm going to keep looking till I find him. Do you want to come with me?"

"Yes, please," said Kitkat. Her fear had faded and the colour had come back into her face. She trotted after Ben.

19

They didn't see the monkeys again. Nor did they find the lion, if that was what they'd heard. But they did discover a road running through the middle of the forest. They stood in the shelter of the trees, not wanting to venture into the open till they'd decided which way to go, left or right. Both directions looked the same. There was no reason to choose one over the other.

They'd been standing there for a couple of minutes, unable to make a decision, when Kitkat cocked her head on one side and said, "What's that?"

"What's what?"

"Shh!"

Now Ben could hear it too. The sound of an engine. Coming closer.

"Don't move," he whispered. "Don't make any noise."

"Look who's talking!"

"Shut up!"

A moment later, an open-backed truck emerged round the curve and hurtled down the road towards them.

Ben and Kitkat stood very still.

The driver didn't slow down or glance into the trees where they were standing, so he couldn't have noticed them.

Once the truck had passed their hiding place, Ben got a quick glimpse into the back. There, he saw a shaggy black shape. For a moment, he thought it might be a bundled-up carpet or an old bathmat. Then his mind registered that it was actually a large monkey sprawled in a heap. The monkey had black fur and a long tail. It might have been unconscious or dead. Before Ben had a chance to see whether the monkey was breathing, the truck had gone.

He looked at Kitkat. From her excited expression, he could tell that she had seen the monkey too.

"Was that it?" she said. "Was that your monkey?"

"No, mine was smaller. And brown, not black."

"You're sure?"

"Of course I'm sure," said Ben. "I know what he looks like. That was a completely different type of monkey."

"So there's your monkey. And this monkey. And those other monkeys. And the lion. That's. . ." Kitkat counted on her fingers. "That's four monkeys and one lion. What's going on here?"

"I don't know," said Ben. "But we're going to find out. Let's follow the truck."

He stepped out of the trees and on to the road. Kitkat hesitated. Curiosity pulled her one way, fear another. It didn't take long for curiosity to win the struggle. She hurried after her brother. Ben waited for her. When she reached him, they walked along the road together, heading in the same direction as the truck.

Kitkat said, "It must be a zoo."

"If there was a zoo here, we'd have heard about it," said Ben.

"It must be private."

"Can people have private zoos?"

"If they're rich enough," said Kitkat.

"We'd still have heard about it."

"If I was a millionaire, I'd have my own zoo. I'd fill it with elephants. Do you think we'll find elephants in this zoo? That would be so cool!"

Kitkat hurried forward, jogging along the road. "Elephant! Elephant! Where are you?"

"You're mad," said Ben. "You should be locked up."

Kitkat took no notice. She jogged up the road, calling out to any elephants who might be lurking in the woods. "Hello? Elephant? Come out, come out, wherever you are!" Then she stopped and stood very still, listening intently.

Ben stopped too. "What is it?"

Kitkat listened for a moment longer, then looked at him with big eyes. "There's another car coming."

Now Ben heard the engine too. It was heading towards them, coming from the direction that the van had gone.

"We've got to hide," he said. "Come here!"

Kitkat ran to meet him. He waited till she reached him and then, together, they sprinted into the undergrowth.

Just as they reached the trees, a white Land Rover came racing round the bend. Ben thought they'd been quick enough, but he was wrong. With a piercing squeal of brakes, the Land Rover screeched to a halt. A door swung open and a deep male voice shouted, "You! Stop!"

Ben leaped over a branch and dodged deeper into the undergrowth. Behind him, he could hear the same voice shouting more aggressively: "Don't you move! Stop right there!"

And then there was the sound of Kitkat's voice, crying out, calling to him: "He's got a gun!"

Ben whirled round and looked back the way that he had come.

Kitkat was right. Through the trees, he could see the silhouette of a man standing by the side of the road and the outline of his gun, the barrel pointing into the air.

If Ben had been alone, he might have kept running, confident that no one would actually take a shot at him. Not here. Things like that didn't happen in the middle of the English countryside. But he could see the forlorn shape of his little sister, standing between him and the gunman, not daring to move.

He couldn't leave her.

He trudged back the way that he had come. Branches crackled underfoot. He emerged from the trees and stepped on to the tarmac.

A tall, thin man was standing beside Kitkat. He had a shaved head and a mean face. He was wearing sturdy black boots, green combat trousers and a camouflage jacket.

He was holding a high-powered rifle with telescopic sights.

Lucky I didn't run, thought Ben. With a gun like that, you'd never miss your target.

Nearby, the Land Rover was parked in the middle of the road, its engine still running.

Ben walked along the road till he reached his sister. She was biting her lower lip. She looked scared. He grinned at her, hoping she couldn't see from his face how nervous he was really feeling, then stared defiantly at the soldier. If he *was* a soldier. That was certainly what he looked like. The Land Rover, the gun, the uniform – what else could he be?

The soldier stared back. He seemed even more surprised to see them than they were to see him. He scowled at the two children, his eyes wandering over their clothes and faces, and then he said, "Are there any more of you?"

"No," said Ben. "Just us."

"You'd better not be fibbing."

"It's the truth," said Ben.

"I hope so. Who are you? What are you doing here?"

"We're not doing anything."

"You must be doing something. You're here, aren't you?"

"We're going for a walk."

"Oh, you just walked in here, did you?"

"Yes."

"Come off it. You can't just walk through a ten-foot-tall steel gate. How did you really get in?"

Ben didn't answer. Nor did Kitkat. Neither of them wanted to give away the secret of their ladder.

"Trespassing is illegal," said the soldier. "If you don't tell me what's going on, I'll take you straight to the police. You know what they'll do? They'll put you in a little cell and they'll slam the door and they won't let you out till you start talking. Would you like that?"

"No," said Kitkat. It was the first word that she'd spoken and she looked surprised by the sound of her own voice.

"You've got to choose," said the soldier. "Either you tell me what you're doing here or I'll take you to the police. Which would you rather?"

"We'll tell you," said Ben.

"That's a good decision, that is. You will tell the truth, won't you?"

"Yes, sir."

Ben was surprised to hear himself address the man as "sir", but it must have been the right thing to do, because the man nodded approvingly. "Go on, then. How did you get in here?"

"We climbed over the wall," said Ben.

"How'd you do that?"

"With a ladder."

"A *ladder*." The soldier shook his head. "I don't believe this. We spend thousands on security and what happens? A couple of kids climb over the wall with a ladder. What am I going to do with you?" He looked at Ben and Kitkat for a moment, then clicked his fingers at them. "Come on," he said, gesturing at the Land Rover. "You'd better get in."

"Why?" said Ben.

"We're going for a drive."

"Where?"

"Wait and see." The soldier fingered his rifle. "Go on, get in."

Ben walked towards the car, but Kitkat lingered behind.

"You too," said the soldier. "Get in."

"I'm not allowed to," said Kitkat.

"Says who?"

"My mum."

"Does she now? And where's she?" The man looked around, pretending to search the woods for any sign of someone hiding there. "I can't see her."

"She's not here," said Kitkat. "But she told me never to get in a car with a stranger."

"What's your name?"

"Katherine."

"Let me tell you something, Katherine. You're on private property. What your mum says – that doesn't count for nothing here. If I tell you to get in the car, you get in the car. Do you understand what I'm saying?"

"Yes," said Kitkat in a small voice.

"Good." The soldier opened the door. "Get in then."

Kitkat glanced at Ben. He nodded. She clambered into the back seat. Ben followed her.

The soldier slammed the door after them. He got into the driver's seat, did a three-point turn in the middle of the road and headed back in the direction that he had come from.

Ben glanced at Kitkat. She was sitting forward, her shoulders hunched, staring with a fixed expression at the back of the seat ahead of her. Ben whispered, "Kitkat?"

She glanced at him. "Yes?"

"You OK?"

"I'm fine. How are you?"

"I'm fine too."

"Good." Kitkat gave him a quick smile, then turned her attention to the back of the seat in front of her, staring intently at the wrinkled material as if it held the answers to all her questions.

From her expression, Ben could tell she was scared. *Me too*, he wanted to say. But he didn't say a word. He just stared at the road ahead, waiting to see where they were going.

20

The road emerged from the trees and entered a wide expanse of farmland. Up ahead, Ben could see an old house and two big barns. They must have arrived at Hunchback Farm.

The farm was surrounded by a metal fence, about the height of a man. At regular intervals along the top of the fence, there were floodlights and CCTV cameras, watching the road, the grass and the trees. No one could have come close without being seen.

That's interesting, thought Ben. There's a wall already. Why do they need this fence too? Are they keeping people out? Or keeping people in?

It's a farm, he reminded himself. And farms have animals. That's why they need a fence.

But do farms usually have floodlights and cameras? Are farms guarded by soldiers with rifles? Why would a farm need so much security?

They stopped at a metal gate which looked strong enough to stop a bulldozer. The driver got out and opened the gate, then drove through and shut it behind them. The whole procedure took so long that Ben had enough time to study the cluster of CCTV cameras attached to a pole beside the gate. They looked modern and sophisticated. One of the cameras was leering directly down at him. He stared into the black lens and wondered who was staring back at him.

They drove towards the farm.

Several old cars and vans were parked in the yard. Ben recognized one of them as the truck that he and Kitkat had seen earlier on the road. It was empty. There was no sign of the dead or unconscious monkey which had been lying in the back.

A young man came out of the nearest barn, carrying a heavy bucket in each hand. He was followed by a black dog.

The man was wearing black wellies, blue dungarees and long plastic gloves. He had a long, lean face and black hair. As he walked across the muddy farmyard towards the Land Rover, he noticed the children sitting in the back. He was obviously surprised to see them. He called out to the driver, "What have you got there? A couple of cheeky little monkeys?"

"Very funny," said the driver. "Where's Mum?"

"She's cleaning out that dead one's cage. The one who died yesterday. You know which I mean?"

"Yeah, yeah, I do. Thanks, Fred. See you later."

"You certainly will."

The man and the dog stood in the middle of the farmyard, watching them leave.

They drove past the barns and rejoined the road. No one spoke. Ben had all kinds of questions that he wanted to ask, but he thought it was wiser to keep quiet.

The road curved. They reached a group of scruffy old Portakabins. Ben could see more cameras fixed to trees, walls, posts and the Portakabins, watching whatever happened. You couldn't move without being filmed. This wasn't an ordinary farm. Whoever lived here must be paranoid about intruders. But why? What was happening here? It didn't look like an army camp either. There weren't any jeeps or tanks. The man in the farmyard hadn't even been wearing a uniform. So what was this place?

They left the road and drove across the grass, passing several Portakabins. As far as Ben could see, they looked no different from the Portakabins that you might have found on a building site, a carpark or even a school playground, used as an extra room.

Every Portakabin looked the same. They had two strong bolts on the doors, so they could be locked from the outside. Thick wire mesh covered the windows. Muddy paths led between them, showing the routes that men must have walked every day.

Ben was staring at the Portakabins, wondering what they were for, when he saw what looked like a face, pressed against the wire mesh that covered one of the windows. It appeared to be staring directly at him.

The Land Rover was bouncing around on the rough ground, jolting its passengers from side to side, so Ben couldn't really get a good look, and then, before he could be sure of what he'd seen, the face had dropped down from the window and disappeared.

What had it been? A man or a monkey? Or nothing? Ben peered through the window, scanning that Portakabin and the others, hoping to see another face, but only blank windows peered back at him.

One of the Portakabins had an open door. That was where they stopped. The driver got out of the car and went inside.

Ben sniffed the air, then wished he hadn't. Kitkat put her hand over her nose. There was a terrible smell. Like a blocked drain. Or a loo that hasn't been flushed for a week.

A small old woman scurried out of the Portakabin and marched to the Land Rover. The driver hurried after her, protesting and waving his arms, but she took no notice.

The old woman had white hair and wrinkled skin, browned by long days spent working outside. She was wearing black wellies, a thick green skirt, a baggy blue jumper and an old anorak. She put her face close to the glass and peered through the window at the two children.

Ben studied the old woman's features. She had bloodshot eyes and a sour expression, as if life had dealt her many disappointments. She must have been about sixty, if not even older, but her strong face radiated energy and determination.

She turned round to confront the driver. "You idiot," she snapped. "Why did you bring them in here?"

"I said I was sorry." The driver shrugged his

shoulders. Suddenly, he looked like a small boy, making excuses to avoid a punishment. "I didn't think it would matter."

"Damn right you didn't! You never think! That's your problem, Jacob Skinner. Always has been. When are you going to learn to think for yourself?"

"It won't happen again."

"That's what you always say." Turning her back on him, the old woman opened the Land Rover's door. She looked at the two children. "Come on then. Out you get. Let's be seeing you."

Ben and Kitkat reluctantly clambered out of the car and stood before her. She inspected their faces as if she was searching for something. Ben and Kitkat stared back, trying not to show any hint of the fear that they were both feeling.

Ben knew he couldn't escape. He'd have to leave Kitkat behind and he wasn't going to do that. Even so, he felt like running. He didn't like the look of the woman in the blue jumper. She wasn't a soldier, he knew that much. But who was she?

She said, "What are your names?"

Ben knew he had to answer for them both. "I'm Ben," he said. "This is my sister Katherine."

"Where are you from?"

"London."

"Come a long way, haven't you?"

"We're staying in Quarryman's Cottage."

"You're on holiday?"

"Yes."

"And you decided to climb over the wall, did you?"

"Yes."

"Why did you do that?"

"We just wanted to go for a walk."

"With a ladder? Over a wall?" The old woman shook her head. "Do you think I'm stupid?"

"No."

"Then don't treat me like an idiot. There are signs everywhere along that wall. If you really climbed over, you must have seen them. You knew you were breaking the law. Trespassing is no different to theft. You do know that, don't you?"

"Yes."

"Thieving – is that what you were doing? Looking for something to steal, were you?"

"No."

"Then you won't mind if we search you."

Ben glanced at Kitkat. He could tell that she did mind. A lot. But they didn't have any choice. "You can search us if you want to," he said. "But we haven't stolen anything."

"I hope you haven't," said the old woman, peering at them with a hard look in her eyes. She nodded to Jacob, who stepped forward and searched the two children, patting them down, then ordering them to empty their pockets.

"And the bag," said the old woman. "Don't forget the bag."

Jacob pointed at Ben's backpack. "Go on, then. Give me that."

Ben took off his backpack.

Jacob tipped its contents on to the grass, spilling apples, plums, cherries and cashews into the mud. He turned the empty bag inside out and ran his fingers along the seams, searching for hidden pockets.

The old woman nudged the fruit with her wellies, then looked up at Ben. "What's all this?"

"Our lunch," said Ben.

She nodded. "You can keep it. Go on, give him his bag back."

Jacob handed the backpack to Ben, who knelt on the grass and bundled the fruit inside. He stood up and slung the backpack over his shoulders.

"Let's get going," said the old woman. "I've got a lot to do today. I wasn't planning for trespassers." She opened the driver's door, then stared at the children. "What are you waiting for? Get in."

Kitkat said, "Where are we going?"

"I'm taking you home," said the old woman. "Unless you'd rather walk."

"We don't mind walking," said Ben.

"I bet you don't," said the old woman. "But you've done enough walking. Go on, get in the car."

They didn't have any choice. They did as they were told.

Jacob sat in the passenger seat. The old woman drove.

As the Land Rover headed back towards the farmhouse, Ben looked through the back window and stared at the Portakabins. He looked at the nearest, then the furthest, and then cast his eyes at each of them in turn, searching for something, anything, although he wasn't sure what.

That was when he saw them.

The same black face. The same small eyes. Pressed against the wire mesh. Staring back at him.

But not just one face.

Six.

He couldn't quite believe it. He wanted to nudge Kitkat and tell her to turn round, but he knew he had to keep quiet. He didn't want Jacob and the old woman to know what he'd seen.

Better if they thought he didn't have a clue what was going on.

The car was bouncing around. The faces were a long way off and, every second, they were getting further away. But it didn't matter. He could see them clearly enough to know what they were.

Six black monkeys, their faces pressed against the wire mesh.

21

They took the same route back to the farmhouse, out of the gate and into the forest. Soon, they were surrounded by trees.

Ben remembered what the old woman had said.

I'm taking you home.

He didn't believe her. Where was she really taking them?

What would he do if the car stopped in the middle of the woods and the soldier reached for his rifle?

Would he have the courage to throw the door open, jump out of the car and run? And what about Kitkat? How would he save her?

He glanced at his sister. She was slumped in her seat, biting her lip, lost in thought. *We'll be OK*, Ben wanted to say, but he didn't dare speak. He stared through the windscreen, watching the road ahead, waiting to see where they went.

The road wriggled through the woods. Soon, they passed the place where the soldier had found them. Not much further, they came to the wall. Their way was blocked by a tall metal gate.

Three metres from the gate, an electronic keypad was attached to a wooden post. The old woman leaned out of the window and typed in a code. The gate opened. They drove through. Behind them, the gate swung shut.

Ben looked back. Fixed to the wall beside the gate, there was a bell, an intercom and a small metal plaque engraved with two words: HUNCHBACK FARM.

They sped down the road, driving alongside the wall.

Opposite the lane that led to Quarryman's Cottage, the old woman stopped the Land Rover. She turned and looked at the two children sitting on the back seat. "You're telling me this is where you climbed over the wall?"

"Yes," said Ben.

"You know what's strange? I can't see any ladders. I don't think you've been telling the truth."

"It must be there," said Ben. "Unless someone's stolen it."

The old woman looked at Ben for a moment,

deciding whether to trust him; then she opened her door. "Come on, then. You show me how you got over the wall."

Ben clambered out of the Land Rover and hurried across the grass to the wall. And there it was. Half-hidden by nettles. The ladder. He called to the old woman, "It's here."

When the old woman came to look at the ladder, she seemed almost disappointed, as if she would have preferred Ben to have been lying. She summoned Jacob. Together, they effortlessly hauled the ladder out of the grass and slid it into the back of the Land Rover.

Ben remembered how heavy the ladder was. And how he and Kitkat had struggled with it. The old woman must be much stronger than she looked.

They got back into the Land Rover and drove up the lane that led to Quarryman's Cottage. As they approached the house, Ben and Kitkat could see a figure sitting on the grass, reading a book.

Harmony was surprised to see a car coming up the lane, but even more surprised when she noticed who was inside. She shut her book and hurried across the grass. Looking through the Land Rover's window, she ignored the old woman and interrogated the two children in the back. "What are you doing? Where have you been?"

"There's no need to shout," said the old woman. "We're right here."

Harmony didn't like being told what to do. She said, "Who are you? Why are they in your car?"

"You know them, do you?"

"Of course I know them. That's my brother and my sister. Can you please tell me what's going on?"

"Where's your dad?" said the old woman.

"California."

"Your mum, then."

"Why don't you just tell me what's going on?"

"If you don't mind, I'd rather talk to your mum."

"Fine. I'll fetch her."

Harmony hurried indoors, irritated that anyone should think that she was less competent or intelligent than an adult.

They waited in silence. Ben and Kitkat glanced nervously at one another, wondering what might happen next.

A minute later, Harmony came back.

"She's busy. She says, can you come back later. And she says, if you're selling something, we're not interested, thank you very much."

The old woman reached inside her anorak and

produced an old leather purse. She opened it, rummaged around inside, and pulled out a creased white card, which she handed to Harmony. "Give that to your mother, please, and ask her to come out right now. You can tell her, if she doesn't want to, I'll have to come in and get her."

Harmony glanced at the card and read what was written on it. If she was impressed, she didn't show it. Without another word, she went back into the house.

She'd only been gone for a few moments when Jennifer emerged from the front door and marched down the path to the car. Her lips were pursed and her eyes were flashing. When she was angry, she was scary. Placing her hands on the Land Rover's roof, she leaned down and spoke to the old woman through the open window: "Good morning, Mrs Skinner," she said. "You've come from the farm, have you?"

"That's right," said the old woman. "I've got two of your—"

"I hope you don't think I'm rude," interrupted Jennifer. "But I'm awfully busy. Would you mind coming back another time?"

"I couldn't do that," said the old woman.

"I'm afraid you're going to have to," said

Jennifer. "If you could come again at a more convenient time, I'm sure we'll have lots to. . ." Her voice faltered. For the first time, she noticed two small people sitting on the back seat. "Ben?" she said. "Katherine? What are you doing in there?"

"Are these your children?" said the old woman.

"Of course they are. What's going on?"

"Nice of you to let them wander round," said the old woman. "Not every mother would like her children trespassing on private property."

"Trespassing?" said Jennifer. "I thought everything on this side of the wall was public land."

"You're right. It is. But they weren't on this side of the wall."

"What do you mean?"

"I mean exactly what I said. They've been trespassing. They used a ladder to climb over the wall and get on my land. They were lucky not to be shot by my boy here. Are you telling me you didn't know where they were?"

"I don't understand." The defiance had gone from Jennifer's voice. "I thought they were reading in the garden."

The old woman smiled. "Tricky little creatures, children. Turn your back for a moment and they've gone."

"It's quite unlike them," said Jennifer. "Ben and Katherine are normally so well-behaved."

"That's the way with children," said the old woman. "I've got four of my own and they're no different. Even Jacob here. . ." She jerked her thumb at the tall, thin man sitting beside her in the passenger seat. "Even he goes off sometimes. But he's old enough to look after himself. I'm not sure if your two are."

"I'm terribly sorry," said Jennifer. "I really can't understand it. I told them very clearly where they could and couldn't go."

The old woman smiled again, more broadly this time. "From London, are you?"

"Yes."

"Having a good holiday?"

"Very nice, thank you."

"I'm glad to hear that. I wouldn't want to spoil it. I don't like the police any more than you do. But I can't have people trespassing on my land."

"You don't have to worry about that," said Jennifer. Her voice sounded ominous now. She looked at the two children in the back of the Land Rover and fixed them with a steely glare. "They won't do it again."

22

Jennifer invited the Skinners to stay for a cup of tea. Jacob looked tempted, especially when he heard that Harmony had baked a chocolate cake, but Mrs Skinner refused for both of them, saying that they needed to get back to the farm as quickly as possible.

Jennifer led Ben and Kitkat into the house and sat them down at the kitchen table. For what seemed like a very long time, she looked at them without saying a word.

Ben and Kitkat kept quiet too. The two of them stared at the wooden tabletop and waited to hear their mother's verdict.

Eventually Jennifer sighed and shook her head. "I don't want to punish either of you," she said in a weary voice. For a moment, Ben felt a great gasp of relief, and then his mother continued, "But I'm going to have to."

123

You don't, Ben wanted to say. You really don't. But he knew better than to talk at a moment like this.

"Before we discuss your punishment," said Jennifer, "I want to know what's been going on. Tell me, Benjamin. And Katherine. What on earth do you think you were doing?"

"We went for a walk," said Ben.

"Over the wall? With a ladder? What kind of walk do you call that?"

"We didn't think anyone would mind," said Kitkat.

They both smiled, trying to look innocent, but Jennifer wasn't convinced. "You knew you weren't allowed to climb over any fences – or the wall. If you wanted to walk further, you should have asked me for permission. Or you should have gone with Harmony. You're much too young to wander off on your own. You did both know that, didn't you?"

Ben and Kitkat nodded.

"I'll tell you what I don't understand," said Jennifer. "You're sensible. Both of you are. And intelligent. And, most of the time, well-behaved. What made you think of climbing a wall and trespassing on someone else's property?"

Ben couldn't think of anything to say. Beside him, Kitkat was quiet too.

Jennifer sighed. "If you don't tell me what's really going on, I can't help you."

They stayed silent.

"Then I will have to punish you," said Jennifer. "I'd rather not, darlings, but you haven't given me much choice."

"We've been looking for the monkey," blurted out Kitkat.

"Shut up," said Ben.

But it was too late.

Jennifer crossed her arms over her chest. "Oh, dear," she said, shaking her head slowly from side to side. She looked at Ben. "This is your fault, is it? You persuaded your sister to climb over the wall?"

"No," said Ben.

"He didn't," said Kitkat. "He told me to stay here. But I wanted to see the monkey."

"I've had enough of these stories about monkeys," said her mother. "It might seem funny to you, but it's not funny for me. You've embarrassed me. You've made me look like a bad mother. Do you know what's even worse? You've made me think I probably am a bad mother."

"Mum, you're—" started Kitkat, but got no

further before Jennifer cut her off, saying she didn't want to hear any more excuses from either of them.

Ben and Kitkat sat in silence, awaiting their punishment.

"I suppose I've learnt a lesson," said Jennifer. "You're both too young to be trusted. You've been behaving like irresponsible little children, so I'm going to treat you like that. You are both confined to the house. You can't go into the garden without my permission."

"What are we going to do all day?" said Ben.

"I'm going to give you some homework," said Jennifer. "You're going to learn French."

"French?" squeaked Kitkat. "But I'm only seven!"

"That's the perfect age for learning languages," said Jennifer. She would provide them with textbooks, she explained. They would have to memorize lists of vocabulary and the conjugations of irregular verbs. She would test them on what they had learnt.

It is always better to accept your punishment in silence. Arguing invariably makes things worse. Kitkat knew that. But she couldn't prevent herself from crying out, "That's so unfair!"

"Life isn't fair," said Jennifer. "Particularly not to children who steal ladders, climb over walls and trespass on other people's private property. Now, you can both go upstairs. I'll bring your French books in a minute." She clapped her hands. "Go on! Upstairs! I don't want to hear another squeak out of you till supper time."

23

La ciboule, le concombre. Onion, cucumber.

Ben sat on his bunk, a book open on his knees, trying to learn lists of French nouns and verbs.

La tomate, le radis. Tomato, radish.

The lines of words blurred and swam before his eyes.

Le brocoli, le poireau, les haricots verts. Broccoli, leeks, beans.

He couldn't think straight. He was distracted by two different noises. The first was the tapping of Frank's fingers on the keyboard. The second was the tinny beat of Frank's music, seeping through his headphones. Both noises were intensely annoying, but the combination of the two was much worse than either of them would have been individually. Just when Ben started to forget one of them, he noticed the other.

La jambe, le genou, le pied. Leg, knee, foot.

Ben wondered whether to say something to Frank. Ask him to be nice, for instance. Ask him to have some consideration for other people and turn his music down. Or even ask him to leave the room. Frank was allowed to go anywhere in the house or the garden and didn't have to stay here. But Ben didn't say anything. He just tried to pretend that Frank didn't exist.

La main, le doigt, l'ongle. Hand, finger, nail.

This is pointless, thought Ben, pushing the book aside. I don't want to learn French. I hate French. Why would I ever want to go to France? I'd rather learn Chinese.

He lay down on his bunk and thought through the events of that morning, trying to make sense of what had happened.

He tried to piece together everything that he knew about the Skinners. He had changed his mind about Jacob and no longer thought he was a soldier. Jacob was a farmer, just like his mother. But what were they doing on their farm?

He remembered all the monkeys that he had seen with Kitkat. Two in the quarry plus one in the back of the truck plus six in the Portakabin. Which made nine. Plus the one who had stolen the strawberries. A grand total of ten monkeys.

He thought about the strawberry thief, the monkey that had started this whole thing. How was he connected to the Skinners? Was he now locked inside one of the Portakabins? And if so, how could Ben ever hope to get him out again?

He remembered the roar that they had heard when they were walking through the woods. Had that really been the noise of a lion? Were the Skinners keeping lions as well as monkeys?

Why would a family of farmers keep monkeys in Portakabins?

These and many more questions crowded into Ben's mind, but he couldn't find any answers. He felt as if he were looking at the pieces of a jigsaw puzzle spread across the floor, searching for some hint of what the final picture might look like. But it was hopeless. However hard he looked, he couldn't even see two pieces which fitted together.

All he knew was this: something was going on, something important, something which linked the strawberry thief, those other monkeys, the lion and the Skinners, and he wanted to know what it was.

And then he had an idea. What if the monkey wasn't in Hunchback Farm? What if the monkey was actually still in the quarry?

As soon as that thought had entered his mind,

he knew he was right. He remembered the trail of banana skins that led him to the quarry. He remembered Kitkat saying, "The caves will still be there later, but the monkeys won't." That was it! He knew where his monkey was. He'd known it all the time. Now he just had to get over the wall again and find him.

He swung himself out of his bunk and clambered down the ladder. When he reached the floor, he glanced at his stepbrother. Frank was lying on the bottom bunk, staring at his computer, and didn't even bother looking up.

Ben opened the door. He glanced both ways, checking his mother wasn't anywhere near. She'd kill him if she caught him out of his bedroom. He couldn't hear anything. She must have been downstairs, concentrating on her work. He tiptoed along the corridor and knocked on his sisters' door.

He heard Harmony's voice: "Come in!"

Ben opened the door. Harmony was lying on one bed, reading a novel, and Kitkat was sitting on the other, hunched over a book of French vocabulary. "Hello, sisters," whispered Ben, not wanting his voice to carry downstairs. "Are you having fun?"

They both replied that they were.

"That's great," whispered Ben. "Kitkat, can I talk to you?"

"What do you want to talk about?"

"It's private. Come out here."

Harmony said, "Is it about the monkey?"

"No, no," said Ben. "The monkey was just a story. He doesn't really exist. This is about something completely different." He beckoned to Kitkat. "Come on! Come out here!"

Kitkat started to stand up, but Harmony put her hand on her arm, holding her back. "You don't have to pretend," said Harmony to Ben. "Kitkat told me everything. I'm sorry I didn't believe you before. But I do now."

Kitkat glanced from her brother to her sister and back again. She said, "I didn't mean to tell her, I really didn't, but it just slipped out. You don't mind, do you?"

Ben stepped into the room, closed the door behind him and stared at Harmony, inspecting her expression. Was she teasing him? If he believed what she said now, would she play along for a while and then turn on him, laughing at his stupidity?

When you have two sisters, you learn to be careful.

He'd have to take the risk. Without Kitkat's help,

he couldn't do anything. If Harmony helped him too, things would be even easier.

Ben said, "You won't tell Mum, will you?"

Harmony solemnly promised that she wouldn't tell her mother or anyone else about the monkey.

Ben sat on the floor between their beds and told them why he was here. He started by describing how he had looked through the Land Rover's window and seen the six monkeys locked inside one of the Portakabins. Then he explained what he'd decided to do and why.

"I can't be exactly sure what's happening inside Hunchback Farm," he said. "But I know enough to know I don't like it."

"Me neither," said Kitkat.

"Shh," said Harmony. "Let him talk."

"Thank you," said Ben. "This is what I know. The Skinners are keeping monkeys in Portakabins. I think they're keeping lions too. I don't know why. But that's not really important. What matters is saving the strawberry thief. He must have escaped from them. I don't want him to get caught again. I'm sure he's living in the quarry. He's not safe there. He can't have anything to eat. That must be why he came and stole the strawberries. If he can't get any more, he'll have to search for food somewhere else.

And if we don't rescue him, he'll get caught and put back in a cage. I want to climb over the wall, go to the quarry, find him and bring him back here. We can give him a home. I can't get over the wall unless someone helps me with the ladder, because I can't carry it on my own. I need your help. But if Mum catches me – or you – she'll kill us. So what do you say? Do you want to risk it?"

He looked at his sisters, suddenly worried that they might turn him down or, even worse, threaten to tell Jennifer.

They both nodded.

"I'd like to help," said Harmony.

"Me too," said Kitkat.

"Excellent," said Ben. "It's too late to do anything now. We don't want to get stuck in the quarry in the dark. But we'll head over there tomorrow morning as soon as Mum starts work."

Kitkat said, "Shall we ask Frank too?"

"No way," said Ben.

"Why not?"

"He's a freak."

"No, he's not."

"He is."

"He's not."

"You can stay here with him if you'd rather."

"No, thanks."

"Then let's stop wasting time talking about him. OK?"

"I guess," said Kitkat.

"Good," said Ben. "Now, this is what we're going to do."

24

In the morning, Jennifer was delighted to see that the children had decided to behave themselves.

Some children might have sulked, she thought to herself. Others might have moaned or begged or tried to persuade their mother to change her mind. But not Ben and Kitkat. No, they didn't indulge themselves in any of those silly antics. They got up early. They ate breakfast together. And then, like little angels, they trooped back to their bedrooms, determined to spend their days doing something useful. Before going upstairs, Kitkat even proved how much French she'd learnt by saying, "*Au revoir, maman. À tout à l'heure.*"

As Jennifer carried her cup of coffee into her study, she couldn't help smiling. She had been a little too harsh, she thought. Ben and Kitkat might have misbehaved, but they weren't bad children. She'd let them spend the rest of the day learning more French vocab and then tonight, during supper, she'd tell them that they'd served enough punishment. Of course, she'd leave the threat hanging over them. If they were naughty again, they'd have to go back to learning irregular French verbs. But if they behaved themselves, they could put away their textbooks and start enjoying a normal summer holiday.

She closed the door of her study and sat down at her desk, looking forward to a full day of uninterrupted work. She switched on her computer and took off her rings. Jennifer hated wearing jewellery while she typed. Every morning, when she sat at her desk, she placed her rings in a small wooden bowl beside her computer, where they sat, glistening in the sunlight, till she finished her day's work. She took a sip of coffee, hunched over her keyboard and started typing.

Jennifer had already written two books, but neither of them had sold more than a few copies. She hoped her third would be a best-seller. It was a manual for living in what she called "an unclear family".

Jennifer liked to say that there are two types of families. She described them as nuclear families and unclear families.

All nuclear families are alike, she said, but every unclear family is unclear in its own particular way.

Nuclear families have a mother and a father and two or three children. They all live in the same house. They all have the same surname. They are a unit.

Unclear families aren't units. They have several surnames and often live in lots of different houses.

Some unclear families have two parents, but others have one or three or four and sometimes even more. Unclear families don't just have a mother and a father, they have stepmothers and stepfathers and girlfriends and boyfriends and partners and ex-partners. Unclear families have children and stepchildren and half-siblings. In an unclear family, all these people live together or apart in an infinite variety of different ways.

Jennifer was writing a book about an unclear family that she knew well. She hoped that, with the help of her book, other unclear families could learn how to live happier, healthier lives.

As her children had already guessed, she was writing about her own family. She promised to change everyone's names and identities, but none of them were fooled. They knew they would be recognized by anyone who read the book.

Kitkat was delighted that she was going to be in a book and Ben claimed not to care, but Harmony was horrified. She hated the thought of other people knowing their business. She begged her mother to stop writing. "These are our lives," she said. "Why do you have to tell the whole world about them? Don't you understand the meaning of the word 'private'?"

Her pleas had no effect. Jennifer just laughed and replied, "You shouldn't be embarrassed, sweetheart. You should be proud!"

Every day, Harmony hoped Jennifer would come to her senses, but it hadn't happened yet. Every day, Jennifer wrote more than the day before. If she carried on working at this rate, she'd finish her book before the end of the month.

25

Upstairs, Harmony, Ben and Kitkat had congregated in the girls' bedroom, directly above their mother's study.

Harmony sat on one bed, Kitkat sprawled on the other and Ben lay on the floor, his ear to the wooden boards. When he heard the sound of typing, he lifted his head and nodded to the others.

Harmony looked at her watch.

They stayed in their positions, not moving, not talking, just listening, for three minutes. Then Harmony whispered, "Let's go."

They knew their mother's habits. Once Jennifer started work, she never stopped before lunch time, when she would go into the kitchen and eat some salad or a bowl of soup. Unless something went horribly wrong on the other side of the wall, they would be back before that.

Harmony opened the door. In single file, they

tiptoed along the corridor and down the stairs. A floorboard creaked. They stopped and stood very still, waiting for their mother to come rushing out of her study and investigate. After a few seconds, Ben nodded at the girls and they kept walking.

They went into the kitchen. Ben opened his rucksack. He'd already packed his camera and a bottle of water. Now, he filled the rucksack with food. He took the same fruit that he'd taken yesterday and brought back again: the two apples, the three plums and the handful of cherries. He also grabbed some biscuits, several carrots, a bag of raisins, a packet of cashews and the remains of that morning's redcurrants.

They tiptoed past their mother's study. She must have been completely absorbed in her work, because they reached the front door without hearing a shout of "Who's that?" or "What are you doing out there?"

In the hallway, near the front door, old coats and leather collars and metal chains were hanging from a line of wooden pegs.

Ben took the smallest collar and the longest chain. When they found the monkey, he was planning to slip the collar round its neck and bring it home like a dog.

He could already imagine his mother's reaction when she saw the monkey. First, she'd be so surprised she wouldn't be able to speak. Then she'd laugh. Finally she'd turn to Ben and beg his forgiveness for ever imagining that he might be a thief.

There was a torch beside the front door, left there in case anyone arrived at the cottage in the middle of the night and couldn't find the fuse box. Ben switched the torch on and off, checking the batteries, then squeezed it into the top of his rucksack. He fastened the buckle, slipped his arms through the straps and hauled the rucksack on to his back. It was surprisingly heavy.

Harmony opened the front door. They filed outside. Ben closed the door very slowly, shutting the latch with an almost inaudible click.

They walked round the house to the shed. The ladder was there, dumped on top of all the dusty junk, exactly where Jacob and Mrs Skinner had left it.

Ben and Harmony carried the ladder between them. Kitkat trotted alongside, offering words of encouragement. "I could sing," she said. "Would that be useful?"

"Very useful," said Ben.

Kitkat can't have heard the sarcasm in his voice, because she immediately broke into song.

"Sshh!" hissed Ben. "Do you want Mum to hear?"

"But you said—"

"I was joking. If you really want to be useful, you could shut up."

"Fine," said Kitkat. She stomped ahead, kicking any twigs that had the bad luck to be lying in her path. Ben and Harmony followed a few paces behind her, trying not to drop the ladder.

At the end of the lane, they waited in the woods for a minute or two, checking no cars were coming, then hurried across the road.

They propped the ladder against the wall and took turns climbing up. Harmony went first. Ben held the base for her, keeping it steady. When she was safely sitting on the top of the wall, Kitkat climbed up to join her. Ben held the base till she reached the summit, then climbed after his sisters. He had the most difficult climb. There was no one to hold the ladder for him. Even worse, the heavy rucksack on his back threatened to topple him over backwards. But he went slowly and, although the ladder wobbled uncomfortably from side to side, it didn't fall over. From the highest rung, he hauled himself on to the wall and sat between his sisters.

"This is so cool," said Kitkat.

Ben would have been happy to sit there for a few minutes, resting his limbs and admiring the view, but he knew that this wasn't a sensible place to have a break. If a car happened to come past and the driver noticed three children sitting on top of the wall, there'd be trouble.

He and Harmony had already discussed what to do next, but talking about it was much easier than doing it.

They shuffled sideways till they were sitting on either side of the ladder, then lifted it together. The weight was unbelievable. Carrying the ladder had been exhausting, but this was much worse. Their arms hurt. Their legs too. Straining their muscles and gritting their teeth, they hauled the ladder up, up, up, up, up and on to the top of the wall.

For a moment, it balanced there like a seesaw, rocking gently up and down. Then they tipped it forward and let it slide down the other side. The feet slammed into the ground with a loud clank.

They took turns climbing down. Ben went first, so he could stand at the bottom and hold the ladder steady for the others. Kitkat came next. And Harmony last.

They stood knee-deep in the nettles.

Kitkat had worn jeans rather than a skirt, remembering the rash that she'd got last time, and told Harmony to do the same.

Ben grabbed the ladder with both hands and tipped it sideways. He pushed hard to get it moving. Then momentum took over. The ladder skidded down the bricks and disappeared into a thick patch of nettles. It was completely hidden.

"That's perfect," said Ben. "No one will see it there. Come on, follow me." He turned round and trampled through the nettles, breaking the stalks with his trainers, making a path for his sisters. They headed for the quarry.

26

Ben had hoped that they might catch the monkey by surprise, but the only living creature in the quarry was a large crow, who hopped away as the children approached, then lazily flapped his ragged wings and lifted himself into the air.

When the crow had flown over the hill and disappeared, the quarry was empty. Even the banana skin had gone. Some animal must have eaten it.

Ben knelt on the gravel and shrugged off his rucksack. It was a great relief to slip the straps from his shoulders. Without its dead weight on his back, he felt much more energetic. He unfastened the buckle, reached inside and pulled out the cashews, the biscuits and some fruit. He opened the packets.

Kitkat leaned forward with both arms outstretched. "Hmmm, that looks good."

"Don't touch anything!" snapped Ben. "It's not for us."

"Keep your knickers on, I'm only joking."

"Well, it's not funny. Only one person – only one *creature* – is allowed to eat this. Here, take some. But don't eat it."

"I won't," said Kitkat, rolling her eyes.

They each grabbed a handful of fruit, nuts and biscuits. They would use it as bait to catch the monkey.

If Kitkat hadn't mentioned hunger, the thought wouldn't have occurred to Ben, but he suddenly realized he was starving. Tough. He'd have to go hungry. With any luck, they'd find the monkey fast and get home for lunch.

Ben didn't want to lug the rucksack around more than he had to. It was too heavy. He stuffed the rest of the food back inside and fastened the strap. If the crow flew back, it wouldn't be able to get anything.

He dumped the rucksack on the ground and handed candles to his sisters, keeping the torch for himself.

"That's not fair," said Kitkat. "Why do you get the torch?"

"Life isn't fair," said Ben.

"Don't say that. You sound like Mum."

"If you want, we can swap. Here, you have the torch. I don't mind using candles."

Kitkat shook her head. "No, it's fine. You can keep it."

Ben didn't argue. He wanted the torch for himself.

He had brought two boxes of matches. Harmony took both.

"What about me?" whined Kitkat.

"You're too young to play with matches," said Harmony.

"Then how do I light my candle?"

"I'll light it for you."

"What happens if it goes out? I'll be left in the dark. All alone! Do you want me to get murdered?"

"Of course I don't want you to get murdered."

"Then give me some matches."

"You can come with me," said Harmony. "We'll search the caves together. If your candle goes out, I'll light it again. All right?"

Kitkat nodded, not quite sure whether to be pleased or disappointed.

They headed for the three small caves at the far left-hand side of the quarry.

Each cave looked the same. Narrow tunnels

plunged into the rock, vanishing almost immediately into darkness. They might have continued for hundreds of metres. Take a few steps and you would be swallowed by the shadows. Anything might be hiding there: water, a long drop, a dragon, a flock of blood-sucking vampire bats, waiting for a tasty little human to step inside.

Kitkat cupped her hands around her mouth and shouted into the darkness. "Hello?"

The only response was her own voice echoing back at her. "Heellllooo-ooohh-oooohhhh."

She peered nervously into the gloom, then looked at the others. "Maybe this isn't such a good idea."

Ben said, "Are you scared?"

"No," said Kitkat. "I just don't want to be eaten by a lion."

"You won't be," said Harmony. "Here, hold these. Like this."

Kitkat held both candles upright. Harmony struck a match and lit them. The flames wavered in the breeze.

"Look out for any evidence of the monkey," said Ben. "Banana skins, strawberries, whatever. If you find him, shout. But don't let him out of your sight. OK?"

Harmony and Kitkat nodded.

"See you back here," said Ben. "Good luck. Hope you find the monkey!"

"You too!"

"And you!"

They walked into the caves.

27

Ben switched on the torch. The first thing he noticed was the silence. The second was the cold. He hoped the third would be a small brown monkey with a long curly tail.

A sudden movement made him whirl round. His heart was beating fast. For a moment, he couldn't see anything. And then he realized what it must have been. The changing angle of his torch had caused a shadow to race along the wall.

He took a deep breath of the cold air and told himself to calm down. If the monkey was here, he'd have scared it away already.

He walked to the end of the cave, plunging into the depths of the darkness, using his torch to check every crevice, hunting for any sign that the monkey was or had been there.

Near the back of the cave, he thought he saw the shape of a tail, but it was just a crack in the rock.

Finally, reluctantly, he concluded that the cave held only one living creature.

Himself.

When Ben came out of the cave, Harmony and Kitkat were waiting for him. Kitkat was holding a lit candle, cupping her hand around the flame to protect it from the wind. Harmony shook her head, anticipating Ben's question. "Empty," she said.

"Mine too," said Ben. "Maybe we scared him off. We shouldn't have made so much noise."

"He's hiding," said Kitkat.

"How do you know?"

"He's not stupid. He knows we're here. I bet he went into one of the other caves when he heard us coming and he's going to stay there till we go away. If I was a monkey, that's what I'd do."

"Let's hope you're right," said Ben.

They worked their way around the quarry, two caves at a time, Ben in one and the girls in another.

At first, Ben searched slowly and diligently, working his way from one end of each cave to the other, casting the beam of his torch meticulously around the interior, peering into the darkest recesses and hunting for the slightest sign that an animal might have slept or eaten there, but he soon lost both patience and enthusiasm, and sped up. The cold seeped into his bones. His arms ached. Worst of all, he suspected that they were wasting their time. The monkey could be anywhere. Maybe he wasn't in the caves at all. Maybe he was hiding in the forest. He might even have been captured by the Skinners and taken back to the farm.

He did find a couple of interesting things. In one cave, someone had spray-painted graffiti around the walls, drawing pictures and writing names. The paint had faded so much that Ben could hardly make out what they'd drawn and written. In the entrance to another cave, half-burnt logs and blackened stones showed where people had once built a bonfire. It must have been a good place for a barbecue. You could sit there, warmed by the flames of the fire, and watch the sun sinking over the hills of Hunchback Valley.

Humans weren't the only creatures that had left their traces in the caves. Ben saw some black pellets which must have been made by rabbits or deer. Harmony found the white skeleton of a long-dead bird. Kitkat felt something flutter past the back of her head. It might have been a bat, she told Ben, or maybe an owl, although she couldn't be sure, having glimpsed nothing more than a black shape vanishing into the shadows. Harmony had been standing beside her, but hadn't seen or felt a thing.

Some of the caves weren't much more than holes scraped from the rock. Others stretched for three or four metres. They were like full-size rooms with enough space to park a car or build a kitchen. And one, the biggest, was as long and as wide as a gym or a church hall.

Kitkat stopped at the entrance.

"I'm not scared," she said, crossing her arms and staring at Ben, daring him to contradict her. "Give me the torch and I'll go in. But I'm not going in there with a candle. No way, buster."

Ben could see how nervous his sister was and how hard she was trying to hide it. "We'll all go in together," he said. "A cave like that is too big for one person."

They walked inside in a line, Ben in the middle, a sister on either side. The vast cave gulped them into its wide mouth and shrouded them in darkness.

Water dripped down the walls. The stale air smelt of mould and decay. Strange sounds echoed through the gloom. Long slow creaks. The dripping of water on rock. There was a sudden short shriek, followed by a kind of sigh, which

154

might have been a breath or just the breeze, whistling through a hidden window in the rock.

"I don't like this," whispered Kitkat.

Ben said, "Why are you whispering?"

"I don't know," whispered Kitkat.

"Then don't," said Ben. "Talk in a normal voice. You're making me nervous."

"OK," whispered Kitkat, then cleared her throat and said the same word again, much louder. "OK!"

Her voice echoed back from the end of the cave. "OK . . . kay . . . kay. . ."

She grabbed Ben's sleeve and held on tight. On his other side, Ben could feel Harmony, walking so close that their shoulders touched. Together, the three of them walked deeper into the darkness.

Ben lit their way with the torch. The cave was so long that the beam wasn't strong enough to reach the end. Harmony and Kitkat were both holding candles, but they cast so little light that they were practically useless.

Alone, any of them would have turned back by now, but none of them wanted to be the first to suggest giving up.

They reached the back of the cave without seeing any sign of the monkey. Ben cast the torch quickly across the wall to make sure that there weren't any tunnels leading deeper into the rock. He said, "There's nothing here. Let's go back." Together, they turned round and hurried towards the entrance.

Kitkat's candle went out, then Harmony's did too, but it didn't matter. The fierce daylight silhouetted the shape of the cave's mouth, showing them exactly where to go.

They emerged blinking and half-blinded by the brightness. Ben must have been the first to recover his vision, because he was the first to see the monkey. Without even thinking about what he was doing, he ran forward, waving his arms and shouting, "Hey! What are you doing? Get off!"

28

The monkey whirled round and looked up. Red juice spilled from his mouth and dribbled down his chin, staining the soft white fur of his belly.

Ben skidded to a halt.

He realized how stupid he had been. They had made all this effort to find the monkey. And now they'd found him, he was trying to chase him away.

He stood very still, trying not to make a sound.

The monkey stared at him.

Ben stared back.

No one moved.

The monkey was sitting beside Ben's rucksack.

He had unfastened the clasp and tipped out the contents on to the gravel, making a messy pile of plums, apples, carrots, cherries, redcurrants, raisins, biscuits and cashews. He had thrown the camera, the collar and the chain aside, discarding whatever wasn't edible. He had even turned the rucksack inside out, exposing the seams, checking that he'd shaken out all its contents.

Now he had to make a choice. Stay with the food or run away. He hesitated, weighing up his options, looking at the food, then Ben, then the food again, trying to decide what to do.

He must have been fearless. Or very hungry. There were three of them and only one of him, but he decided that the risk was worth taking. He picked up another plum and carried on eating, keeping his eyes fixed on the three humans, waiting to see what they did next.

When Harmony and Kitkat tiptoed forward to join Ben, the monkey kept a careful eye on them and continued eating.

You wouldn't have thought that a little monkey could eat so much. Nor would you have thought that, having eaten the contents of a rucksack, he would still be hungry. But this monkey had a vast appetite. He made his way through the plums, the apples, the carrots, the cherries, the redcurrants, the raisins, the biscuits and the cashews, then picked any crumbs out of the gravel and ate them too. When he was sure that he had finished everything, he approached the three children, wanting to see what they were holding in their hands.

Ben knelt down, put his torch on the ground and stretched out both his arms, palms upwards.

The monkey scrambled in the opposite direction. He must have thought that Ben was going to take a swipe at him. But he didn't go far. After a few paces, he stopped, turned round, and looked back.

Ben hadn't moved. He was kneeling on the ground in exactly the same place. Cupped in his hands, he was holding a plum, some cashews, some cherries, some raisins and three chocolate digestive biscuits.

The monkey stared at Ben. His eyes darted from the food to his face, then back to the food.

No one made a sound. Ben was very careful not to move. He was desperate for the monkey to come closer, but he knew that any movement, any sound, any attempt to communicate, would only drive him away.

The monkey shuffled forward. He was ready to run. If anything had scared him – if Ben had lunged at him or one of the others had made a sudden movement – he'd have been scampering across the quarry before they got anywhere near him.

His eyes flicked from Ben to the food to Kitkat to the food to Harmony and back to the food. Fear told him to retreat. Greed urged him onward. His belly won the battle. He took another small step. And another. And one more. Now he was almost close enough to reach out with one of his paws and grab a biscuit, but he didn't lunge. Not yet. He turned his little head from side to side, checking the three children in turn. And then, trying to take them by surprise, he darted forward, grabbed some cherries from Ben's hands and scrambled back again. When he was a safe distance away, he turned to see if any of the children had followed him.

Kitkat couldn't stop herself smiling, but the others didn't even move that much.

The monkey gulped down the cherries, spat out the stones and came back for seconds. Then thirds. He ate the raisins, the cashews and the plum, leaving the biscuits for last. He snatched one with both paws, lifted it to his nostrils and took a quick sniff. He nibbled a corner. Crumbs spilled down his front. The biscuit must have tasted as good as it smelt, because he scoffed the lot and reached for another.

Minute by minute, mouthful by mouthful, the monkey forgot to be frightened. He squatted comfortably beside Ben, casting inquisitive glances at his shoes, his clothes, his hair and his face, and picking the last crumbs from his palms.

"Someone's coming," said Kitkat.

"How do you know?" said Ben.

"I can hear a car. Can't you?"

Ben couldn't. Nor could Harmony.

The monkey cocked his head on one side, listening. A second later, he whirled round and, without a backward glance, scrambled across the gravel towards one of the caves on the other side of the quarry, leaving a trail of raisins, cashews and biscuit crumbs.

The grumbling engine was getting louder. Now the others could hear it too. A car was coming towards them.

"We've got to hide," said Ben. "Get in the caves! Quick!"

They sprang to their feet and sprinted after the monkey.

Ben hadn't taken more than a couple of paces when he remembered his stuff. "Don't wait for me," he shouted after the others and darted back.

He could hear the engine clearly now. It couldn't have been far away. Any moment now, a car was going to drive into the quarry. They'd see him immediately.

He scrabbled around on the ground, grabbed the chain, the collar, the camera and the rucksack, then ran after his sisters.

He was just in time. As he hurled himself across the gravel and disappeared into the dark entrance of the cave, a white Land Rover drove into the quarry.

29

The Land Rover drove across the quarry and stopped roughly where Ben had dumped his rucksack. The driver's door swung open. Jacob Skinner got out. He was carrying a rifle.

If Ben had left anything behind, Jacob would spot it immediately. He would see a plum or a water bottle. And he'd know someone else had been here.

Jacob walked to the front of the Land Rover and looked around the quarry, staring at the gravel, the boulders, the half-demolished buildings and the caves. He was holding his rifle close to his chest, one hand on the barrel, the other on the stock. He could have lifted it to his shoulder in an instant and fired off a shot.

Ben stood very still. He was hidden. Jacob couldn't have seen him. And yet he didn't feel safe. He couldn't help worrying that his presence could somehow be sensed.

Behind him, Harmony and Kitkat had retreated into the safety of the shadows. He could hear their breathing. It sounded very loud. *Keep quiet*, he wanted to say. But he knew he was being crazy. Sounds wouldn't travel beyond the cave's entrance. Out there, standing in the middle of the quarry, there was no way Jacob could hear the sound of a breath.

When Jacob had satisfied himself that the quarry was empty, he lowered his rifle to his side, took a final look round and returned to the Land Rover. He got inside and drove out of the quarry on the same rough track that had brought him in.

Ben waited till the noise of the engine had faded, then stepped out of the cave and looked around the quarry. He couldn't see the monkey.

He knew where it had gone. One of the caves on the other side of the quarry. He jogged over there, switched on his torch and walked inside. The darkness felt familiar. He walked down to the end and back again, scouring the walls with torchlight, but there was no sign of any living creature.

His sisters were waiting for him outside the cave.

"Hurry up," called Harmony. "We've got to get out of here before they come back!"

"What about the monkey?" said Kitkat.

"He's gone."

"You don't know that." Kitkat turned to her brother for support. "We have to stay here, don't we?"

"Actually," said Ben, "I think she's right. We should get out of here." He knelt on the gravel and packed his rucksack more securely, then pulled the straps tight and swung it on to his back. "Let's go home. It's lunch time and I'm hungry."

Harmony took one last look around the quarry and whispered, "Bye, monkey. Good luck. Wherever you are."

They set off at a quick pace, walking along the track and keeping their eyes fixed on the trees, searching for any sign of the returning Land Rover.

Ben realized Kitkat wasn't walking with them. He turned round. She was standing exactly where they had left her. Her arms were folded. There was a defiant expression on her face. She said, "What?"

"Aren't you coming too?" said Ben.

"No."

"Why not?"

"Because I'm staying here. Someone has to protect the monkey from those people."

165

"Good luck," said Ben. "Did you happen to notice Jacob's rifle?"

"Of course I did."

"How are you going to protect the monkey from that?"

"I'll be OK," said Kitkat. "I've got a black belt in karate."

"You've got a black belt in being annoying," said Ben. "Come on, stop mucking around. We're going home. All of us. You can't stay here on your own."

"Don't tell me what to do," snapped Kitkat. "You're not a grown-up. If I want to stay with the monkey, I will."

"Fine," said Ben. "When it gets dark and the lions come out – and the rats – don't come crying to me for help."

"I won't," said Kitkat, although she sounded much less sure of herself now. She bit her lower lip.

If she stayed here alone, she'd have fun for the rest of the day, searching for the monkey and perhaps even finding him, but what would she do at night? What if there really were lions here? And rats. . . And vampire bats. . . And other, even wilder beasts, which hid during the day and emerged at night, searching for food. . .

"Let's all go home together," said Harmony, her

voice soft and reassuring. "The monkey can look after himself. Remember how fast he ran when he heard the car? He'll be fine for one more night."

Had Ben said the same words, Kitkat wouldn't have taken any notice, but she trusted her big sister. She cast a wistful glance at the caves, hoping the monkey might have come to say goodbye, then trudged across the gravel towards her siblings.

30

They crossed the clearing and waded through the
nettles. Ben was relieved to see that the ladder was
where they'd left it.

Now they just had to get over the wall.

That would be the difficult bit. But they'd done
it once. They could do it again.

Ben leaned down and brushed aside the nettles.
As he reached for the ladder, he heard a noise
behind him. Footsteps. Rustling grass. Someone
was running after them.

Jacob? Mrs Skinner? Or. . .

He wheeled round. For a second, he couldn't see
anything or anyone. Just trees and grass and
nettles. He turned his head quickly from side to
side, searching for the source of the noise. And then
he glimpsed a familiar shape. Lurking in the long
grass, there was a small brown monkey with a long
curly tail.

Harmony and Kitkat turned to see what he was staring at.

"Aahhh," said Kitkat. "He's so sweet."

"What are we going to do with him?" said Harmony.

"Nothing," said Ben.

Kitkat stared at her brother. "What do you mean 'nothing'?"

"I mean nothing," said Ben.

"Shouldn't we look after him? Shouldn't we help him?"

"He doesn't need our help," said Ben. "If we told him what to do, he wouldn't take any notice. Let's just go home. If he wants to come too, he will."

While Ben and Harmony hauled the ladder out of the nettles and leaned it against the wall, the monkey scrambled up a nearby tree and perched on a low branch. He sat there, scratching his ears and watching them intently, as if he had never seen anything so curious.

Ben held the ladder. Harmony climbed first. Kitkat went next. When they were sitting side by side, Ben climbed gingerly up the ladder and joined his sisters on the top of the wall.

The monkey swung himself through the high branches of a tall tree, leaped across the wall and scrambled into the branches of another tree on the other side of the road. Gravity meant nothing to him. He went where he wanted, treating the world like his own personal playground.

Compared to the monkey, Ben felt useless. His arms were short and weak. His legs were inflexible. His feet were flat. He had no tail. Even with the help of a ladder and both his sisters, he took ten minutes to accomplish what the monkey had done in one graceful leap.

Humans are hopeless, thought Ben. I'd rather be a monkey. We might be able to drive cars and fly planes and send rockets into space, but who cares? Wouldn't it be better just to jump through the air like that?

They hauled the ladder over the wall and climbed down. The road was empty. Harmony and Ben carried the ladder up the lane. Kitkat closed the gate and hurried after them. The monkey went ahead like a scout, stopping every few moments to look back and check that they were following him.

They dumped the ladder in the woods. They could come back later and sneak it into the shed.

"I'm going to fetch Frank," said Kitkat. "He should see this."

"Don't bother," said Ben. "He'll just say, 'I'm not

interested in monkeys, I'd rather play with my computer.'"

"I'd like to ask him anyway," said Kitkat. "If you don't mind."

"Do what you like."

"Then I will," said Kitkat. "It's not fair to leave him out."

She jogged towards the cottage.

Ben was wrong. As soon as Frank heard that there was a monkey in the garden, he switched off his computer. He must have wondered if Kitkat was playing some kind of game, but he followed her anyway. She led him out of the house and through the garden. When he saw the monkey, his face broke open with a big smile. None of them had ever seen him look so happy.

"That's the coolest thing," said Frank. "I've never seen a capuchin before."

Kitkat said, "You've never seen a *what*?"

"A capuchin."

"What's a capuchin?"

"He is," said Frank. "Haven't you ever heard of capuchin monkeys?"

"I've heard of cappuccinos," said Kitkat. "Does that count?"

"Kind of. They're both named after Capuchin monks. They wear brown and white robes. That's why cappuccinos are called cappuccinos and capuchin monkeys are called capuchin monkeys."

"How do you know all this?" said Kitkat.

"I know all kinds of useless stuff. It just seems to get stuck in my brain." Frank smiled self-consciously, then sat down on the ground and stared intently through his thick glasses at the monkey. "Hello, little fella."

The monkey glared back and joggled nervously from side to side, ready to scramble up a tree if the new arrival made any unexpected movements. He had grown used to the three small human beings, but he wasn't sure whether to trust a fourth. Especially one who was taller than the others and had those strange round reflective eyes.

Frank said, "They're supposed to be the most intelligent monkeys in the world."

"What about chimps?" said Ben. "Chimps can do sign language. And maths."

"Chimps aren't monkeys," said Frank. "They're apes."

"What's the difference?"

"Monkeys have tails, apes don't. We're apes. More or less. So are chimps, gorillas, gibbons and

172

orangutans." Frank grinned. "You see? More useless information."

"I think it's interesting," said Kitkat.

"Interesting stuff is usually useless," said Frank. "And useful stuff is usually boring. That's what I've found, anyway. Like this monkey. He's one of the most interesting things that I've ever seen, but he's not exactly going to be useful for anything, is he?"

"He must be useful to someone," said Ben. "Or why would the Skinners keep him on their farm?"

31

The monkey was lying down, dozily watching the children through half-closed eyes. They were talking loudly, but he wasn't scared. He felt full and sleepy. Over the past few days, he couldn't have eaten much more than a few bananas and strawberries, but this morning he'd stuffed his belly. Now he was content to sprawl on the grass in the warm sunshine and enjoy a well-earned snooze.

If he had understood what the four children were saying, he would have paid more attention to their conversation. They were discussing why the Skinners could possibly want to keep monkeys and lions in a secret encampment, miles from anywhere, down a road that led nowhere. Someone had invested a lot of time, money and effort into keeping the farm hidden. Casual passers-by would never guess what lay behind the high wall. Whatever Hunchback Farm might be, it wasn't a zoo or a circus. So what was it? Who were the Skinners? Why were they so paranoid about trespassers? What were they scared of?

Frank quizzed the others. He wanted to know what had happened on their visits to the quarry and what they had seen in the farm. They told him everything. He listened mostly in silence, interrupting only occasionally to ask a question, and then he told them what he thought was happening in Hunchback Farm.

"It's the army," said Frank. "They've hired the Skinners to breed monkeys."

According to Frank, who seemed to be an expert on the subject, the army used a lot of monkeys. In the future, they'd use a lot more. Monkeys would take the place of humans.

Scientists would genetically modify monkeys to use as advanced weapons systems. A race of super-monkeys could be equipped with special powers, allowing them to operate machinery, carry bombs, fire guns or even fly planes. By sending them into the battlefield, the army could save the lives of thousands of human soldiers.

"What about the lion?" said Kitkat. "Why would the army want a lion?"

Frank couldn't answer that.

Kitkat had a different explanation. She reeled off a list of celebrities with extraordinary pets. She could name a princess who always bought diamond bracelets for her poodles on their birthdays, a singer who refused to perform unless her chipmunk was in the audience and a film star with a baby leopard. They were the type of people, suggested Kitkat, that the Skinners were planning to make money from. If celebs thought lions and monkeys were the latest trendy pets, they would be queuing up to buy them.

Harmony had another idea. She thought the Skinners were farming exotic animals to sell as high-class delicacies. They probably had all kinds of creatures in the Portakabins, she said. Not just monkeys and lions but porcupines, turtles, emus, alligators, antelopes and anything else that someone might want to eat. They bred them just like pigs or chickens. If you went to the right shops, you could buy lion steaks, monkey kebabs, antelope cutlets and porcupine pies.

While the others were debating these different theories, Ben watched the monkey.

I'm wasting time, he thought.

The monkey wasn't going to be here for very long. As soon as he realized that they didn't have any more food, he would race back to the quarry and seek the safety of a dark cave, a long way from any humans. For the short time that the monkey was actually here, Ben knew he should be taking advantage of his presence.

He stood up and said, "I'm going to fetch Mum."

"Mum?" Harmony looked worried. "Why?"

"She should see the monkey," said Ben. "Then she'll know I'm not the strawberry thief."

"Maybe that's not such a good idea," said Harmony. "She's not going to be happy we climbed over the wall. And she might not be too pleased we've brought back a wild animal."

"Don't worry," said Ben. "She'll be happy about it. Ever since the first strawberries went missing, she's been worried her own son is a thief. Now she'll know I'm not."

"Somehow," said Harmony, "I don't think Mum's going to see it quite like that."

Ben didn't care what Harmony thought. "I'll be back in a second."

Leaving the monkey with his sisters and Frank, he strolled through the garden towards the house, intending to fetch Jennifer and bring her outside. He hadn't taken more than ten paces when he heard the sound of rustling. A few leaves fluttered to the ground. He looked up. Overhead, the monkey was leaping through the trees, keeping pace with him.

"He likes you more than us," said Kitkat.

Ben wondered if that was really true. He didn't think so. More likely, the monkey was just curious. Or hungry. Or. . . Maybe he does like me more than the others, thought Ben. It was a nice idea.

He headed for the house. He remembered walking into the kitchen and telling his mother about the strawberry thief. He still felt annoyed about her reaction. *Either you're a liar*, she'd said. *Or you're a thief*. Now she'd know the truth.

He didn't want her to grovel. A simple apology would be enough. He just wanted her to look him in the eyes and say "sorry".

Ben stopped at the front door. The monkey had scrambled down from the trees and scampered across the grass, coming to a halt no more than a metre from Ben's feet. He sat on the ground, looking up at Ben, his small dark eyes gleaming with intelligence.

Ben said, "Do you want to come inside?"

The monkey didn't reply. Of course he didn't. Monkeys can't talk. But Ben had the strange sense that he could see some kind of response in the monkey's eyes. Something which said: *I want to see what's on the other side of that door*.

Then you can, thought Ben. He opened the door and stepped into the house.

The monkey stayed outside, his head turning quickly from side to side, his eyes glaring into the hallway.

Ben whispered, "Do you want come in?"

The monkey didn't move.

"You're not scared, are you?" whispered Ben.

The monkey stared up at him with a defiant expression as if to say: *Me? Scared? I'm not scared of anything*. He peered past Ben's legs, inspecting the hallway for potential dangers. There was a black umbrella lying on the floor under the coat rack. For some reason, the monkey found it fascinating. Dodging round Ben's legs, he darted into the house and grabbed the umbrella with both paws.

"Come on, then," whispered Ben. "Let's go and meet Mum. But you'd better behave. She doesn't like animals."

Ben walked down the hallway and stopped outside his mother's study. The monkey followed him, dragging the umbrella by its plastic handle, scraping the spokes along the stone flagstones.

From the other side of the door, Ben could hear the sound of his mother's fingers rattling across a keyboard. He knocked twice.

The typing stopped. Ben heard Jennifer's voice: "Yes?"

"It's me," Ben shouted through the door.

"Hello, Benjy! How are you?"

"OK."

There was a short pause, as if Jennifer was waiting for Ben to say something else, and then she must have decided that he wasn't going to, because she started typing again.

Ben put his head closer to the door and spoke through the wood. "Mum, can I talk to you?"

The sound of typing stopped and his mother shouted, "Not now, Benjy. I'm busy."

"It's important, Mum."

"My work's important too."

"But this is *really* important, Mum. I've found the strawberry thief."

"What do you mean?"

"I've got the monkey. He's here with me now."

For a moment, nothing happened. Then, Ben heard the sound of his mother's chair scraping against the floor, followed by her footsteps, coming closer. Jennifer opened the door and looked at him.

"You're not going to start telling those silly stories again, are you?"

"They're not stories," said Ben.

"I've already told you, Benjy, I don't want to hear another word about your imaginary monkey! It's not funny, it's not clever and it's not. . ."

Jennifer's voice faded. Her eyes widened. She had seen the small brown creature that was squatting on the floor beside Ben's feet, clutching an umbrella with both paws. For a moment, she was speechless. And then, in a small voice, she said, "Where on earth did you find that?"

Before Ben could answer, the monkey dropped the umbrella, ducked between Jennifer's legs and charged into her study.

32

The monkey had seen the rings on Jennifer's desk. He couldn't resist their sparkle. He sprang across the carpet, bounded over Jennifer's chair, plonked himself on her keyboard and grabbed a pawful of jewellery.

Jennifer shrieked.

Ben panicked.

The monkey turned round to check what all the fuss was about. Seeing that neither Ben nor Jennifer had come any closer, he turned back again and grabbed a few more rings. As he darted one way, then the other, focusing his attention first on the wooden bowl, then the two humans, checking to see if they moved, his paws pounded on the keys of Jennifer's laptop. A stream of letters raced across the screen. This is what he wrote:

fkgjlhp'orkjl;hkl
][[;'kl\'pl;klkl;kkjljklsdfese:l';l;f
]d[y\'l;\'pdyhm.sen.k,.mlyjkl;'

It might have been a monkey poem made up of monkey words. Or it might just have been nonsense. Whatever it was, Jennifer hated it. She shrieked at the monkey: "Shoo!"

The monkey turned to look at her, decided she wasn't worth worrying about, and plunged his paws back into the wooden bowl. He pulled out a gold ring and lifted it to his mouth.

Jennifer recognized her wedding ring. She turned to her son. "Benjamin! Do something!"

"What do you want me to do?"

"What do you think? Get that animal out of here!"

"Yes, Mum."

"And don't let him eat my ring!"

"No, Mum."

"Because if he does. . ."

She left the threat hanging in the air, not bothering to explain exactly what horrible punishments would be inflicted on her son.

It didn't matter. Ben could fill in the gaps for himself. No pocket money. No going out. No fun.

He'd be confined to his bedroom for the rest of the summer with a French dictionary, learning every word from *aardvark* to *zoology*.

Ben ran towards the monkey, his arms outstretched, hoping to grab him or the ring and perhaps even both.

The monkey was too quick for him. He bounded away, his tail sweeping across the desk, sprinkling the floor with paperclips and scattering pencils in every direction.

If Jennifer hadn't been standing in the doorway, the monkey would probably have sprinted straight out of the room, but she was blocking his path. Instead, he jumped from the desk to the bookshelf, then on to the thick brown curtains, grabbing the material with all four paws.

Ben ran after him.

The monkey hauled himself towards the ceiling.

There was a loud *rrrrriiiiiiiiippp!* Followed by a series of *pop!-pop!-pop!-pop!-pop!*s And the curtain came away from its hooks.

As the curtain crumpled and crashed towards the floor, the monkey leaped upwards and grabbed the rail with both front paws. There he hung, swinging gently backwards and forwards, his tail dangling downwards. He opened his mouth. The wedding ring fell out, dropped through the air and disappeared behind the radiator.

Jennifer ran to rescue it.

The monkey must have thought she was coming for him, because he got out of the way as fast as he could, springing from the curtain rail to a picture frame. It couldn't hold his weight and slithered down the wall. By the time that the frame smashed into the ground, spraying glass across the carpet, the monkey had already flung himself through the air. He swung round a reading lamp, scrambled down the back of an armchair and dodged out of the open door.

Jennifer reached under the radiator and grabbed her wedding ring. Then she raised herself to her full height and glared at her son. She didn't say a word, but she didn't have to. Her expression told him everything that he needed to know.

"I'll get him," said Ben. "Don't worry, Mum, I will."

Not waiting to hear her reply, he sprinted after the monkey.

Jennifer slipped the wedding ring on to her finger and followed her son out of the room.

*

The front door was shut, so the monkey couldn't leave the house. Instead, he ducked into the kitchen.

Ben darted after him. Jennifer followed a couple of paces behind.

They were just in time to see the monkey running along the worktop, scattering knives and spoons and forks, tipping over cups and glasses, knocking the fruit bowl to the floor, and leaping on to the table.

By now, the monkey must have realized that he had misjudged Jennifer. She wasn't harmless; she was scary. He wanted to get away from her. As fast as possible. But there was nowhere to go. She was blocking the door. The kitchen had no other exit. He was trapped. Screeching with fear and fury, he danced backwards and forwards on the top of the table, waving his tiny paws and showing his sharp little teeth, daring her to come closer.

Jennifer was just as furious as the monkey, but she didn't move, not wanting to get scratched or bitten. She stood in the doorway, staring at him with steely eyes.

Ben looked around the kitchen, wondering what to do. He wasn't sure who would win a battle between his mum and the monkey, and he didn't want to find out. Suddenly, he saw a solution. He ran to the kitchen window and opened it, then stepped aside, offering an escape route to anyone agile enough to squeeze through the gap.

The monkey didn't hesitate. He jumped off the table, darted out of the window, sprang into the tree and swung through the branches, putting a safe distance between himself and the kitchen.

Jennifer walked to the window. Outside, she could see the monkey, squatting in the tree. They glared at one another.

Jennifer closed the window, turned her back on the monkey and looked at Ben. "I want the truth," she said. "No stories. No exaggerations. No justifications. Just the truth. Where did you find this monkey?"

Ben told her what had happened.

When Jennifer had heard enough, she sent Ben to join his siblings in the garden and returned to her study. It looked chaotic. The curtain had been torn down. The lamp had been knocked over. Paperclips, pencils, rubber bands, broken glass and books were scattered across the floor. Her computer was covered with coffee. Cleaning up would take ages. But that could wait. First, there was something more important to be done. In the top drawer of her desk, she still had the white card that she had been given on the previous day. She rang the number and said, "Is this Mrs Skinner?"

"Yes. Who's this?"

"Jennifer Fitzroy."

"Who?"

"We met yesterday. I'm staying with my family at Quarryman's Cottage."

"Oh, yes. I remember. What can I do for you?"

"This is probably a very strange question, Mrs Skinner, but have you lost a monkey?"

33

The Skinners' Land Rover stumbled up the lane and parked outside Quarryman's Cottage. Mrs Skinner was driving. She got out first, followed by Jacob, who was carrying his rifle with both hands as if it were a precious object. They looked around the house and the garden, staring at its other six inhabitants – two boys, two girls, a woman and a monkey.

Jacob scowled at the children, but Mrs Skinner only had eyes for the monkey. Shading her eyes from the sun, she peered up into the old oak tree, where he was squatting on one of the lower branches.

Jennifer had been pacing up and down the lawn, waiting impatiently for the Skinners to arrive. As soon as she saw their Land Rover, she marched down the garden to meet them.

Ben had been going crazy with impatience. He

had wanted to warn the monkey to run away, to flee through the forest, to get as far away as possible, but he couldn't say anything because his mother had been watching him. And now it was too late.

The monkey didn't move either. He didn't need to; he was already a safe distance from anyone else. That was what he thought, anyway.

Jennifer thanked Mrs Skinner for coming so quickly.

"I didn't have much choice," said Mrs Skinner. "I need that monkey back again. Dangerous creatures, monkeys. They bite, you know."

"Do they really? He looks so sweet."

"He may look sweet to you, Mrs Fitzroy, but he's got sharp teeth, and he's not afraid to use them. I could show you some scars. So could my sons."

"I'm sure you could," said Jennifer. "I have to admit, I can't imagine why anyone would want to keep a monkey as a pet. Particularly if they bite so much. If you don't mind me asking, why do you do it?"

"They have their charms. Now, if you'll excuse me, Mrs Fitzroy, I'd better take him back home. Take the chance while I can, if you see what I'm saying."

"Yes, of course." Jennifer stepped aside. "Be my guest."

"Thank you," said Mrs Skinner. She took a couple of paces forward and stared at the monkey. She was smiling, but her smile was small and cold, as if she were meeting an old friend whom she no longer liked.

The monkey stared back at her. If he recognized her, he didn't show it. Nor did he show any signs of fear. He still thought he was safe up there, high above the ground, out of reach of those incapable, earthbound humans. He knew they couldn't climb trees or fly, so how could they possibly catch him?

Mrs Skinner flapped her arm at her son. "Give me the gun."

"Let me do it," said Jacob. He raised the rifle to his shoulder.

"You'll only mess it up."

"Hush, Ma. I'm ready. I'm going to shoot him down."

"Give the gun to me."

Jacob wavered for a minute, wondering whether to defy his mother, then handed over his rifle.

In one swift, sure movement, Mrs Skinner raised the rifle to her shoulder and put her right eye to the sights, taking aim at the monkey. Her finger curled around the trigger. She was just about to shoot when a small girl ran across the grass, planted herself between the rifle and the monkey, and stretched out her arms, offering herself as a target.

"Don't kill him," shrieked Kitkat. "He hasn't done anything wrong!"

Mrs Skinner lowered the rifle, pointing the barrel at the ground, and smiled. "Don't you worry, we're not going to kill him."

Kitkat pointed at the rifle. "Then why do you need that?"

"There are no bullets in this rifle. It's loaded with tranquillizers. Do you know what they are?"

"Like Valium?" said Kitkat.

Mrs Skinner smiled as if Kitkat had made a joke, although she hadn't meant to, and said, "Tranquillizers put you to sleep. If he's awake and he's scared, he'll only do himself some damage. I've seen it happen a hundred times. This is the safest way to catch a monkey, I guarantee you that. If he's asleep, he can't get hurt."

"But why do you have to shoot him?"

"It's not like being shot. He won't feel a thing. He'll just nod off. Don't you understand?"

"No."

"You will. Let me do my business and he won't be hurt, you'll see."

Kitkat stared defiantly at Mrs Skinner. She sounded very sensible. Perhaps she was even telling the truth. But Kitkat didn't trust the Skinners and hated the thought of them shooting the monkey, even with a tranquillizer. If they wanted to get her out of their way, they would have to come and move her themselves.

Another voice broke the silence.

"Come on, Katherine," said Jennifer. "Do what the woman says."

Kitkat looked at her mother, debating whether to disobey her, then decided not to. What's the point of fighting a battle that you can't win? With her head bowed, she sloped across the grass and took her place alongside her siblings.

Mrs Skinner lifted the rifle, aimed again and fired.

There was a loud bang. The monkey screamed and spun round on the branch, clutching his hip with both paws, then fell out of the tree and plummeted to the ground. He landed in a heap. The fall didn't seem to have hurt him, but the dart had. His body writhed and twisted, dancing in one direction, then another, as if he were trying to get away from the pain, and he uttered a succession of shockingly loud shrieks, each of which sent a jolt through Ben's entire body.

Kitkat put her hands over her ears, then her eyes, but couldn't prevent herself from watching through the gaps between her fingers.

Ben knew how she felt. He didn't want to watch either, but he couldn't not. It was disgusting and, at the same time, it was fascinating. He'd seen animals being tranquillized on TV, but the process always looked straightforward and painless. In real life, being sent to sleep was much more of a struggle. The monkey tried his hardest to stay awake, desperately clinging to consciousness.

As the drug seeped into his bloodstream, his protests faded. The defiance went out of his eyes. His head wobbled woozily from side to side. He staggered. And slumped. And lay down.

There he stayed, his limbs sprawled out, his tiny paws clutching the grass. He shuddered one final time and then he was still.

Mrs Skinner handed the rifle to Jacob and walked across the grass to the monkey. She picked him up by the scruff of his neck and displayed him to Kitkat. "What did I tell you? He's fast asleep."

"You said it wouldn't hurt," said Kitkat.

"It didn't."

"Then why was he screaming?"

"That's just him showing off. Monkeys do that. You don't have to worry, he'll wake up in a couple of hours with a nasty headache, nothing worse." Mrs Skinner turned to her son. "Put him in the car, Jacob. We'd better get this little fellow home."

"Yes, Mum." Jacob took the monkey from his mother and carried him towards the Land Rover, swinging him casually through the air as if he were a rubbish bag.

Mrs Skinner smiled at Kitkat. It was a false smile, worn for Jennifer's benefit, and none of the children were fooled. "He'll be hungry when he wakes up," said Mrs Skinner. "He probably hasn't eaten for days. We'll feed him up, don't you worry."

Kitkat frowned at the old woman, furious about the way that she'd treated the monkey.

Ben could have told Mrs Skinner what the monkey had actually eaten today, but he kept quiet. If she knew his belly was full, she might not feed him again. And food, Ben suspected, was one of the few pleasures awaiting the monkey when he got back to Hunchback Farm.

Mrs Skinner thanked Jennifer again for calling her so promptly, then turned to the four children.

"If I wanted to," she said, "I could ring the police and report what you've done. They'd press charges. No doubt about it. This isn't just trespassing, this is theft." Mrs Skinner paused for a moment, letting her words sink in, then smiled. "But I've agreed not to, because your mother's made me a promise. She says you'll never trespass again. I hope she's right. For her sake. And for yours."

34

As the Land Rover turned the corner and disappeared down the lane, Jennifer ordered the children to go inside. She wanted to talk to them, she said, and the garden wasn't the place for a serious conversation.

In silence, they trooped into the house and sat round the kitchen table. Jennifer followed them. She took a long look at the four children, then sighed deeply.

"I really don't know what to do," she said. "Perhaps you can help me. Try and put yourself in my position. I've trusted you. I haven't placed any restrictions on your behaviour. In exchange for that freedom, I expected you to behave yourselves. I treated you like adults because I hoped you would be able to behave like adults. But you've done the complete opposite. You've taken advantage of the freedom that I've given you. You've trespassed on private property. You've stolen an animal who didn't belong to you. You've embarrassed me. So, please, just tell me one thing. What am I going to do with you?"

Kitkat tried to protest, explaining that they couldn't be accused of stealing the monkey, because he was free already, and they'd actually tried to dissuade him from following them over the wall, but her efforts were useless. She had hardly begun her explanations when Jennifer interrupted her: "That's quite enough. I don't want to hear any more of your ridiculous stories."

"They're not ridiculous!" cried Kitkat. "You've seen the monkey! You know Ben was telling the truth!"

"I said, that's enough. And I meant it. I will not have you shouting at me, Katherine."

"But, Mum—"

"Katherine!"

Kitkat didn't protest again. She dipped her head and stared at the table, hiding the tears that were swelling in the corners of her eyes.

Jennifer turned to her son. "As for you, Ben. . ."

"Yes, Mum?" He tried to sound innocent and eager. As if he was looking forward to learning what he had done wrong.

"I am extremely disappointed by your behaviour," said Jennifer. "Katherine is barely more than a baby. But you should have known better."

"I know," said Ben.

"I said you weren't allowed to leave the house. I was very clear about that. Wasn't I?"

"Yes, Mum."

"So why did you?"

"I don't know."

"You don't know?"

"No."

"Can't you do any better than that?"

Ben shook his head. "Not really, no."

Jennifer sighed. "Oh, Benjy. What is wrong with you?"

"I don't know," said Ben.

He could have argued with her, but he knew he'd just make things worse. Even when his mother was in a good mood, she didn't like people disagreeing with her. Ben bowed his head and kept his mouth shut, hoping she would leave him alone.

To his surprise, it worked. Jennifer switched her attention to the two older children. She spoke to Frank first. "I know you weren't as involved in this as the others," she said. "But I'm afraid you'll still have to take some responsibility for what happened. You could have tried to stop them. You should have come and told me what was happening. Next time, I hope you will."

She paused for a moment, waiting for Frank to respond, but he didn't. He just stared at her, his face blank, his eyes expressionless, as if his body was present but his mind was elsewhere. Jennifer looked at him for a moment, then turned to Harmony. "As for you. . ." Jennifer shook her head. "I can hardly believe what's happened. Is this true, Harmony? Did you really climb over the wall with Ben and Katherine?"

Another girl might have lied or quibbled or tried to wriggle out of the situation by blaming someone else, but not Harmony Elizabeth Amis. She confessed everything.

"Oh, Harmony," said Jennifer in a quiet voice. "I thought you were better than that."

Harmony was in shock. For her, this was an entirely new experience. She was never told off, because she always behaved better than anyone in the family, parents included. Now, not only finding herself the subject of a telling-off, but knowing that she'd done wrong and therefore deserved it, she had no idea what to say.

Jennifer looked around the table at the four

children, then sighed. "I'm going to ring your fathers," she said. "There's going to have to be some kind of punishment for this, although I don't yet know what. I'll discuss that with Jeremy and Robert. For now, I'd like you to make me a promise. I want you to promise to behave. All four of you. Do you promise?"

"I promise," said Harmony.

"I promise," said Kitkat.

"I promise," said Frank.

"I promise," said Ben.

"Thank you," said Jennifer. "Now you can go to your rooms."

The children left the table and trooped silently upstairs.

When their footsteps had faded and the house was quiet, Jennifer went into her study. She searched under a pile of papers and found the phone.

She tried to ring Jeremy in Beijing. There was no answer. She left messages on his mobile and at his hotel, asking him to call her as soon as possible.

She could have rung Robert in Los Angeles, but she didn't really feel like talking to her ex-husband. She knew what would happen. A discussion about the children would quickly develop into an argument and, within moments, they'd be shouting at one another. She would call him tomorrow when her feelings had softened. He could talk to Ben and Harmony. He might even be able to make them see some sense. They had a surprising amount of respect for their father's opinion.

Jennifer sat down at her desk. She stared at the chaos that surrounded her and wondered how she was going to survive the next three weeks, trapped in a tiny cottage in the middle of nowhere, looking after four impossible children.

35

It's my fault, thought Ben.

I'm a fool. I'm a failure. I've done everything wrong.

It's all my fault.

He was lying on his back on the top bunk, staring at the ceiling and wondering how he could have been such an idiot.

He had been lying there for a long time, but he didn't feel like moving. He didn't really feel like doing anything.

Underneath him, Frank was on the lower bunk, doing exactly what he always did. Typing fast on his computer while listening to loud music through his headphones.

Frank didn't seem bothered by what had happened.

Fair enough, thought Ben. Why should he be? He hadn't stolen a ladder, trespassed on private property or taken a monkey without the owner's consent. He'd just watched what the others were doing. If there was any justice in the world, he wouldn't be punished.

Things were very different for Ben.

He had messed things up. Not just for himself. For everyone.

He felt sick with guilt.

He thought about the ways in which life would be better if he hadn't interfered. For the monkey. For Kitkat. For Harmony. Even for Frank. He didn't yet know how Jennifer was going to punish them, but he was quite sure that the rest of the summer was going to be miserable.

He had ruined their holidays, but he'd done something even worse too: he had lured the monkey out of the quarry, where he had been free to roam where he wanted, and thrust him back in the hands of the Skinners.

He remembered how the monkey had looked, swinging through the trees, grabbing branches with his arms and legs and tail, and the envy that he'd felt, his desperate desire to be as acrobatic and free as that. Now the monkey would be locked inside one of the Portakabins on Hunchback Farm. He would probably be sharing the cramped space with a group of other monkeys. He would see nothing except the view through a small, square window covered with wire mesh. That would be his entire existence. From now till the day that the Skinners decided to sell him, kill him, eat him or do whatever they did with the animals on their farm.

He remembered how the monkey had looked when he was lying unconscious in the back of the Land Rover. Ben just got a quick glimpse before Mrs Skinner drove down the lane, but that had been enough to fix the image in his mind.

The monkey's floppy limbs were splayed in every direction. His mouth was open. A line of saliva dribbled from his gums. His eyes were open too, but they stared sightlessly into the distance. He might have been dead. And if he wasn't, he would be soon.

These thoughts had been running round his head for a long time, dragging him into a deep depression, when a voice broke the silence.

"I've found your monkey."

The voice came from the lower bunk.

Ben didn't react immediately. He had no idea what Frank meant and couldn't decide if he cared enough to find out. Curiosity eventually drove him to poke his head over the edge of his bunk and look down at his stepbrother. He said, "What?"

"I said I found your monkey."

"What are you talking about?"

"You heard me. If you're not interested, that's fine."

Frank had taken off his headphones to talk to Ben. Now he put them back on again, cutting himself off from the world, and devoted all his attention to his computer.

Ben flopped back on his bunk and stared at the ceiling.

I found your monkey.

What did that mean?

Maybe Frank was just mucking about.

No, that didn't seem very likely. Frank wasn't the mucking-about type. He couldn't exactly be called a joker. Which made the whole thing even more bizarre.

Ben rolled off his bunk, clambered down the ladder and sat on the edge of Frank's bed. He waited for a moment, but Frank didn't react. He waved his hand in front of Frank's face.

"Yes?" said Frank.

"I did hear what you said. I just don't understand what you meant. What were you talking about?"

Without a word, Frank pressed a few keys on his laptop, then turned it to face Ben.

The whole screen was taken up by a black and white photograph of the monkey. Of course, it could have been another monkey which looked exactly the same as Ben's, although he could hardly imagine that two creatures could look so similar. Not only did the monkey in the photo have the same funny little clump on the top of its head, but the same alert, inquisitive expression in its eyes.

Ben said, "Where did you get that?"

"I hacked into their servers and pulled the images from their CCTV footage."

"You did *what*?"

"You're doing it again," said Frank. "You're pretending to be stupider than you actually are. It's a very annoying habit."

"Sorry," said Ben. "I didn't mean to be annoying. But I don't understand what you're talking about."

"Which bit don't you understand?"

"Well. . . I suppose I do understand, but. . . You really hacked into their computers?"

"Yes."

"And you got the footage from their cameras?"

"Yes."

"How?"

Frank gave a modest shrug of his shoulders. "It's not so difficult if you know what you're doing."

"But we're not even connected to the internet here."

"I am."

"How?"

"Like I said, it's easy if you know what you're doing."

Ben was quiet for a moment, pondering what Frank had said, and then he asked: "Do you mean you can see everything that happens in there?"

"Not everything," said Frank. "But a lot."

"So where's the monkey?"

"I'll show you."

Frank pressed another key on his laptop. The screen changed. The picture of the monkey was replaced by another black and white image. But this wasn't a still photograph. It was moving footage streamed from a camera.

"That's one of their CCTV cameras," said Frank. "Here's another." He pressed the key once more, switching views, and then again and again, moving from one camera to the next.

Ben stared at the screen, hardly believing what he was seeing.

Frank had gained access to the footage from

every camera in Hunchback Farm. By moving from one to the next, he could travel through the entire place and see what was happening everywhere. He could move along the line of cameras on the fence that surrounded the farm or look down from the roof of the barn. He could follow a car as it drove from the farmhouse to the Portakabins. He could track the progress of Mrs Skinner as she walked out of a doorway, carrying a rake under her arm, and headed into the trees. He could see everything that happened inside Hunchback Farm.

He kept his best trick for last.

"Look at this," said Frank.

He pressed another key. The screen went dark.

"What am I supposed to be looking at?" said Ben.

"Can't you see it?"

"No."

"Look at the screen. What can you see?"

"Nothing."

"Look again."

Ben leaned forward and peered at the screen. Dark shadows slowly organized themselves into shapes. He guessed what he was looking at. He said, "Are there cameras inside the Portakabins?"

"There must be," said Frank.

"But what's that?"

"What do you think?"

"I don't know," said Ben, but as soon as he spoke the words, he understood what he was looking at. "It's a monkey."

"Try again," said Frank.

"I can see! Yes! It's two monkeys."

"Try again."

"That's not possible."

"Oh yes it is."

"There must be ten of them!"

"More like twenty."

Frank and Ben sat in silence, staring at the screen. There wasn't much light. The cameras were shoddy. The picture was low quality. But none of that mattered. They could still see enough to understand that they were looking at a crowd of monkeys, crammed together in the Portakabin like commuters inside a train at rush hour.

It's amazing, thought Ben.

I've known Frank all my life. Till today, I've never really wondered who he was. Or what he was thinking.

I could have asked him. But I never bothered. I never cared.

Now I wish I had.

Under those headphones, behind those thick glasses, there might actually be someone quite interesting.

36

Ben and Frank tiptoed down the corridor to the girls' bedroom, trying to make as little noise as possible, hoping they couldn't be heard from downstairs. They weren't exactly sure what would happen if Jennifer caught them, but they knew it wouldn't be pleasant.

Ben knocked softly on the door. There was no answer. He opened the door and went inside.

Harmony and Kitkat were lying on their beds, sick with gloom. When the door opened, Harmony was too depressed to raise her head. Kitkat glanced at Ben and said in a sad voice, "What do you want?"

Ben waited till Frank was inside the room, then closed the door and whispered, "We've got something to show you."

"Don't bother," said Kitkat. "We're not interested."

"We're going to show you anyway," said Ben. "It'll only take a second."

Harmony sat up. "Are you deaf? She said we're not interested."

"You will be," said Ben.

"No, we won't."

"Yes, you will."

"Oh, stop it, Ben. This isn't a pantomime. If you've come to cheer us up, that's very kind, but we don't need cheering up. We just want to be left alone."

"I haven't come to cheer you up," said Ben. "I've come to tell you what's happened to the monkey."

That got them interested. Kitkat wrapped herself in her duvet and shuffled down to the end of the bed. Harmony sat cross-legged in the lotus position. They waited for the show to begin.

Ben cleared a space on the dressing-table, pushing aside the small city of tubs, tubes and bottles that the girls had built in the short time since they'd arrived in the house. Frank opened the lid of his laptop, angling the screen to face the room.

Ben sat beside Kitkat and nodded to Frank. "When you're ready, maestro."

"All systems go," said Frank and pressed a key on his computer.

The screen went black. A picture appeared.

"Is that your monkey?" said Kitkat.

"If you shut up and listen," said Ben, "you'll find out."

For the second time that day, Frank described what he had found. He took the girls on a guided tour of Hunchback Farm. He started with the cameras that were attached to the gates and the fences, watching whoever came in and out. Next, he showed them the farmhouse and the barns, before leading them into one of the Portakabins.

"That's him," said Frank. "That's the strawberry thief."

"No, it isn't," said Kitkat. "That's just a blank screen."

"Look again."

Kitkat scrambled forward, coming close to the screen, peering into the shadowy darkness and trying to make out what was hidden there. She squinted and stared, then said, "You mean that?"

"Exactly."

"Oh, yes. That's his head. That's his tail. Look! Look! He's moving."

Harmony moved forward too. They stared at the

screen, watching the strawberry thief as he moved around his prison, rolling across the floor, then sitting up and scratching his head with both front paws.

Frank took them into every Portakabin. Some were empty, most held a handful of monkeys, and a few were packed so tightly that the miserable creatures hardly had room to move. The strawberry thief appeared to be the only one in solitary confinement.

When Frank finished his lecture, he pressed another key, darkening the screen, then crossed his arms over his chest and looked at Harmony and Kitkat, waiting for their reaction.

Harmony always preferred to think before speaking, but Kitkat was the opposite. "This is terrible," she said. "I feel sick. All those monkeys! It's disgusting! I knew that woman was evil. I could see it in her eyes. We can't let her get away with it! We have to do something! We have to tell someone!"

"Like who?" said Ben.

"How about Mum? No, all right, not Mum. What about the police? Why don't we ring the police?"

"They won't believe us," said Ben.

Kitkat didn't argue. She knew her brother was right. "But we've got to do something," she said. "We can't just let them do that to those monkeys. We have to stop them. I'm right, aren't I? You know I am. So, what are we going to do?"

"Rescue him ourselves," said Ben.

"How are we going to do that? How can we get in there? What about the cameras? Won't they see us?"

"If you stop talking so much, I'll tell you exactly what we're going to do."

Kitkat took a deep breath, slumped back on her bed and pulled her duvet around herself. "Go on, then."

Ben explained his plan.

When he finished, there was a moment's silence, and then Kitkat said, "Mum will kill you."

"No, she won't," said Ben. "She'll just ground me. Or make me learn French. Or stop me watching telly till Christmas. She's not actually going to kill me. But Mrs Skinner really is going to kill the monkey. That's why we've got to stop her."

"She said it was going to be well looked after," said Harmony.

"Do you believe her?"

Harmony would have liked to say yes, but she

couldn't bring herself to lie. She slowly shook her head.

"We have a simple choice," said Ben. "Either we rescue him. Or he gets shot. And this time, Mrs Skinner won't just use a tranquillizer. His life is in our hands. What do you want to do?"

"Of course I don't want a monkey to be killed," said Harmony. "I wish I could come with you. But I can't."

"Why not?"

"I made a promise to Mum."

"You could break it."

"No, I couldn't."

"She'd never know."

"That's not the point."

"What is the point?"

"A promise is a promise," said Harmony. "When you've made one, you can't break it."

"I've broken promises," said Ben. "And the sky didn't fall in."

"You can do what you like," said Harmony. "But I'm different. I keep my promises."

"So do I," said Kitkat.

Ben realized there was no point arguing. Harmony would never knowingly do anything which she thought was immoral. And he couldn't really criticize Kitkat for wanting to be as honest as her older sister.

He did persuade them to do one thing. They agreed to get up at dawn and help him with the ladder. They could do that much without feeling that they'd broken their promise. Then they would come back home. And Ben would be on his own.

37

Ben's alarm bleeped at 5.25 in the morning. He woke up with a jolt of terror. For a second, he didn't know why he was so scared. Was someone in the room? Had he just emerged from a nightmare? And then he remembered what he had to do this morning. The fear returned, stronger this time, like a big hand pressing him into the sheets.

He might have sounded confident when he was explaining his plan to the others, but he felt quite different when he thought about it himself.

He switched off the alarm.

The room was quiet. His head rested on the soft pillow. It would have been so easy to go back to sleep.

I can't do that, thought Ben.

I got the monkey locked up. Now I've got to get him out again.

He pushed aside his duvet, clambered down the ladder and woke Frank.

While Ben got dressed, Frank sat up in bed, opened the lid of his laptop and started work. By the time that Ben was ready to leave, Frank had hacked into the servers and checked that he could still control the flow of information to and from the Skinners' cameras. To his relief, he saw that he could. The system was letting him in. The plan should work.

"Bye," whispered Ben.

"Good luck," whispered Frank.

"Thanks."

There was nothing else to say. Ben picked up his shoes and headed for the door. He stood in the corridor for a moment, checking for noise, hoping his mother wasn't awake yet, but the house was quiet. He tiptoed down the corridor to the girls' bedroom.

They were already dressed and waiting. Ben had worried that Harmony might have had second thoughts, but he should have known that she would never change her mind about anything so important.

The three of them sneaked out of the house and into the woods. Harmony and Ben lugged the ladder down the lane and propped it against the wall.

Harmony and Kitkat held the base of the ladder. Ben started climbing. As he reached the top of the wall, he felt the sun's warmth on his face. It was just appearing over the top of the trees.

He looked down at his sisters. "See you later."

The girls waved.

"Be good," said Kitkat.

"Be careful," said Harmony.

Ben would have liked to say something clever back again, but he couldn't think of anything to say, so he just pulled himself on to the top of the wall. He knew he shouldn't give himself time to hesitate, so he slid forward and plunged straight down the other side.

A shout came from the other side of the wall. "Are you OK?"

Ben recognized Harmony's voice. "I'm fine," he shouted back. "I'm going to start walking. See you later."

He could hear their shouts of "Bye", "Bye" from the other side of the wall. He walked briskly across the clearing towards the quarry. The girls would hide the ladder, then go back to bed. They would return at nine o'clock in the morning. If he wasn't there, waiting for them, they would come back every hour throughout the morning. If he hadn't returned by lunch time, they would confess everything to Jennifer and ask her to call the police.

Ben checked his phone. As he'd expected, it had no reception. In the gloom, the screen cast a bright light and when he looked up, he could hardly see his surroundings. For a second, he felt scared, wondering who or what might be watching him, and then his sight flowed back again. He knew where he was. No one would be watching him, he told himself. No one was awake at this time of the morning. He started walking, rubbing his hands together to get some warmth back into them.

He followed the same route as yesterday.

Dawn arrived. The air was clear. Birds sang in the trees. If he hadn't been so nervous, he might have thought it was beautiful.

He came to the edge of the woods. Up ahead, he could see the fence. There was no way that he could climb over. He would have to go through the main entrance – the same way that he had gone in the Land Rover when he and Kitkat were captured.

He went as close as he could without leaving the shelter of the trees. He could see the gate. It was closed. He had no idea what the Skinners did at night. They might have patrolled the perimeter, watched the cameras or left the farm unguarded, relying on floodlights, cameras, tripwires and sensors to do the job for them.

He stood there for several minutes, watching and waiting, checking for signs of life, but nothing moved.

There were several CCTV cameras fixed to a pole beside the main gate. One of them was pointed in his direction.

He stepped out of the trees, placing himself directly in the camera's path, and lifted his right hand. He waved. Then he jumped back again, hiding himself in the trees.

He had only shown himself for a couple of seconds, but anyone looking at the footage transmitted from that particular camera would have seen him.

He'd just have to hope that Frank was watching. And the Skinners weren't.

He started counting. "One Mississippi. Two Mississippi. Three Mississippi. . ." Frank said half a minute would be enough, so he kept counting all the way to "Thirty Mississippi." Then he took a deep breath, stepped out of the trees and sprinted towards the gate.

38

After helping Ben with the ladder, Harmony and Kitkat had been planning to go back to bed, but they didn't feel tired. It was hours earlier than they normally got up, but sleeping would have been impossible. They were too anxious and too excited.

They crept along the corridor and went into the boys' bedroom.

Frank was sitting on his bunk with his laptop resting on his knees. The glowing screen lit up his face. He looked at the girls and whispered, "Did he get over the wall?"

Harmony nodded.

Kitkat whispered, "Have you seen him yet?"

"No," said Frank. He glanced at the clock in the corner of the screen. "He'll be at least ten more minutes."

Harmony said, "Do you mind if we wait here?"

"You can do what you like," said Frank.

Harmony and Kitkat perched on the bed, one on either side of Frank, and stared at the screen.

They sat there for a long time, watching the footage from one particular camera, till they began to wonder what had happened to Ben. Where could he be? Had he got lost? Or had an accident? What if the Skinners had caught him already?

On the screen, leaves swayed in the breeze.

A skinny boy suddenly darted out of the trees and stood in the middle of the road. He raised his right hand and waved at the camera.

"Look who's here," whispered Frank.

Before the words had left his mouth, the boy on the screen had jumped back into the trees and disappeared. The whole thing happened so fast that, if you hadn't been waiting for it, you wouldn't have noticed anything.

Frank got to work. He wanted to type as fast as possible, but he knew he couldn't make a single mistake or the whole plan would be ruined. Typing with one finger, pressing a single key at a time, he wrote the password that he'd broken last night.

He looked at Harmony and Kitkat, then whispered, "I hope this works."

Harmony nodded. "Me too."

Kitkat bit her lip. She was too nervous to speak.

They both watched Frank as he placed his forefinger on the return key and gently pressed it down.

The screen flashed up a message:

WELCOME FREDERICK SKINNER

"We have lift-off," whispered Frank.

He hunched over the keyboard, typing as fast as he could. The Skinners' computer system opened up to him. He raced through screen after screen, altering options and changing the settings.

It didn't take long. He had been working for less than half a minute when the screen went black.

Harmony said, "Was that meant to happen?"

"Yup," said Frank.

"You did it?"

"I guess I did."

He pressed a few more keys, shifting the viewpoint around the different cameras in the camp, but nothing changed. The screen stayed black. Every camera in Hunchback Farm had been switched off. Not one of them was transmitting any images.

Harmony said, "What do we do now?"

"We wait," said Frank.

39

Ben closed the gate behind him and ran towards the farmhouse. His plan was simple: he would go to the Portakabins, free the monkey and go home again.

Oh, and one other thing. Not get caught.

He could see the house, the barns and the old cars parked in the farmyard, but no people. No one was awake yet.

As he came closer to the farmhouse, a black dog came charging towards him, barking loudly.

Ben didn't know much about dogs. When he was younger, he used to beg his mum to get one, but she always refused and so he stopped trying.

How do you make friends with a dog? How do you stop them biting you? What do you do if one runs towards you, barking and showing its sharp white teeth?

Not knowing the answer to any of these

questions, he just stood very still and waited for the dog to reach him.

That must have been the right thing to do. The black dog barked once more, sniffed Ben's trouser legs, then darted backwards, tail wagging, as if it wanted to play.

"Hello, doggie," whispered Ben.

The dog's tail wagged even faster.

Just as Ben was congratulating himself on making friends with the dog, a loud electronic scream pierced the air. It came from the direction of the farmhouse and sounded like a fire alarm.

The dog whirled round, his ears upright.

In the house, a window lit up. Then another.

Ben could guess what was happening. Switching off the cameras must have automatically triggered an alarm. Frank had warned him that this was a possibility. With any luck, the Skinners wouldn't know how to fix their own computers. Their skills would be no match for Frank's. Even if they were awake, Ben should still have enough time to find the monkey. He would just have to work fast.

He stared at the dog. It looked harmless. Friendly, even. But he wasn't sure. How do you know if a dog is going to bite you? He would have to take the risk. Any minute now, one of the

Skinners might open their curtains and look out of a window.

Ben stepped round the dog and started walking along the road.

The dog came too. It trotted alongside him, its tail wagging, as if they were going for a walk together. It accompanied him past the two big barns and then, without any warning, turned and splashed back through the muddy puddles to the farmhouse.

As soon as the dog was out of sight, Ben started running.

The road curved. He reached several Portakabins. He remembered them from last time. He ran to the nearest. He would check them one by one till he found the strawberry thief.

As he came closer, he put his hand over his nose. The smell was so disgusting that he could hardly bring himself to breathe. An overflowing toilet wouldn't stink so much. But he went gingerly up to the small square window and peered through the wire mesh.

The interior was dark, but he could see enough to know that something or someone was staring back at him. Two tiny black eyes peered out of a wrinkled face, staring nervously at Ben, waiting to see what he would do next. It was a little monkey with skinny arms and a small round skull.

As Ben's eyes adjusted to the gloom, he saw that the monkey wasn't alone and he understood why the Portakabin smelt so bad. There must have been twenty of them crammed into the small, dark, damp space with hardly enough room to lie down or stretch their limbs, let alone run around. They were wallowing in their own dirt. Some of the monkeys were squatting at the sides of the Portakabin, and others were clinging to the ceiling or hanging from the walls, trying to find a scrap of space.

Ben looked around the Portakabin, checking that the strawberry thief wasn't among them, then hurried onward, taking a great gulp of air, trying to wash the foul smell out of his lungs.

He hadn't taken more than a couple of paces when, behind him, he heard a little squeak. He turned round.

One of the monkeys had clambered up to the window and was peering at him, its face pressed against the wire. It squeaked again. The noise was plaintive and desperate. Ben knew what it meant. The monkey was begging him to come back. *Rescue us*, the monkey was saying. *Get us out of here.*

"I'm sorry," whispered Ben. "I can't."

He felt like a brute, turning his back on a helpless creature, trapped in a stinking prison, but he didn't have any choice. If he was going to find his own monkey, he couldn't get distracted by all the others. Not unless he wanted to get caught by the Skinners. He hurried onward. Behind him, the monkey squeaked once more, then was quiet.

Ben went from one Portakabin to the next, peering through the wire mesh windows. There were an amazing variety of monkeys. Big monkeys and small monkeys. Plump monkeys and skinny monkeys. Black monkeys and brown monkeys and white monkeys. But none of them was the monkey that he wanted.

In one of the Portakabins, thirty or forty tiny brown monkeys were heaped on top of one another, crowded together for warmth.

In another, six large black monkeys were sleeping on the floor. They had big faces and strong-looking arms. At first, none of them seemed to notice that they were being watched. And then, just as Ben was turning away, one must have sensed his presence. It sprang to its feet, alerting the others with a loud, angry shriek. They hurtled forward, throwing themselves at the wall, as if they were trying to smash straight through the planks and get at Ben.

He sprang away from the Portakabin, surprised rather than really scared, and hurried onward. Behind him, the monkeys hissed and screeched. He wondered whether they were ordering him to go away or begging him to come back.

The noise alerted the other monkeys in the neighbouring Portakabins. At every window, faces peered through the wire. Paws reached out. Mouths opened. Shrill cries echoed through the air.

Ben tried to ignore the dozens of monkeys clamouring for his attention. He didn't have time to help them. Any minute now, the Skinners might arrive. He ran to the next Portakabin.

And there was his monkey. All alone. Ben had seen lots of other monkeys which looked very similar, but he recognized the quiff, the piercing, intelligent eyes and even the expression on the monkey's face. This one was his.

The monkey knew him too. Some monkeys screamed when Ben peered into their cages. Some hid. A few stood still as if they were hoping not to be noticed. But this one seemed completely confident. He wasn't scared. He remembered the strawberries, the bananas and the rucksack packed with fruit. He knew Ben had come to save him, not hurt him. He sprang to the window, gripping the wire mesh with all four paws, and waited to see what was going to happen next.

Ben slid the long steel bolts and opened the door.

The monkey didn't hesitate. He hopped straight out of the Portakabin and stood on the grass. He could have run away, but he stayed there, looking up at Ben as if to say: *What next?*

"Now we go home," said Ben. "I'm going to get you out of here."

The strawberry thief tilted his head to one side and stared at Ben.

Ben had the strange thought that the monkey was trying to say something to him.

But what?

He suddenly guessed what the monkey wanted to say. He didn't know how he knew, but he did. The monkey was saying: *What about the others?*

"I can't rescue them," said Ben.

He was sure the monkey couldn't understand him. And yet, in some strange way, he felt sure that he knew what the monkey was thinking. The monkey's glistening black eyes weren't just intelligent and inquisitive; they were very expressive too. The monkey was saying: *Why not?*

"Because we'll all get caught," said Ben. "Is that what you want? Would you like Mrs Skinner to put you back in your cage?"

In a very human gesture, the monkey clasped his paws together under his chin and cocked his head on one side. He looked as if he was pausing mid-conversation, taking time to consider what had just been said before he spoke again.

Ben didn't know what to do.

He stared at the Portakabins, thinking about the Skinners and imagining what the monkeys had to suffer. Leaving them here felt criminal. But what else could he do?

His monkey was still squatting on the ground, head cocked on one side, paws clasped under his chin, looking up at him.

"Fine," said Ben. "You win. But I've got to tell you, I think it's a big mistake."

40

Ben struggled with the bolts.

This is crazy, he thought. I'm doing something because I think a monkey wants me to.

At least the monkey was happy. He was hopping back and forth on the grass, waggling his head with excitement and making a series of weird noises – squeals, whistles, hoots and groans – as if he was encouraging Ben to be quick.

I'm being as quick as I can, thought Ben.

On the other side of the door, there were some monkeys. Ben didn't know how many. Nor did he know what they might do when they were released. He tried not to think about that.

He slid back the last bolt and opened the door, then stepped aside, waiting to see who or what would emerge. The strawberry thief squatted on the ground at his feet, keeping up a constant conversation of little squeaks and squeals.

Nothing came out of the Portakabin.

Ben peered through the doorway. Inside, he could see several monkeys squatting on the floor.

They didn't grab their chance to be free. They didn't even move. They simply stared at Ben, waiting to see what this small, skinny human being was planning to do next. Was he coming into the cage? Or delivering food? Why did he smell so different to the men and women who were usually here? And why was he accompanied by an overexcited capuchin who wouldn't stop talking?

One of the monkeys must have been braver than the others. It crept across the Portakabin and peered out of the door, blinking at the sunshine. Then it stopped, stared nervously at Ben and didn't come any further.

Another monkey was a little braver. It pushed past the first one, stepped out of the Portakabin and took a few cautious steps across the grass. There, a noise or a sudden movement must have frightened it, because it whirled round and threw itself back inside, taking shelter in the shadows.

The next monkey was the bravest yet. It peeked out of the door, looking in every direction, checking for danger, and then hurled itself forward. It dodged past Ben, sprinted across the grass to the nearest tree and swung itself into the branches. Dangling by its tail, it opened its mouth and let out a long shriek of joy.

That must have been the signal that the others had been waiting for. They poured out of the Portakabin, splashed through the mud, somersaulted into the long grass and hauled themselves up into the trees. Their fear forgotten, they ran and jumped, shrieked and giggled, somersaulted and leapfrogged, playing around like kids who have been let out of school early.

Ben would have liked to stop and watch, but he didn't have time. There was too much to be done. He ran to the next Portakabin and peered through the window. Inside, he could see six large black monkeys. They looked tough and strong. If they had been feeling aggressive, they easily could have overcome a human being. Ben wondered whether to leave them locked up, not wishing to take the risk that they'd turn nasty, then told himself not to be so cruel. He couldn't release all the monkeys except these six, however harsh they might look. He went to the door and pulled both the long steel bolts.

He needn't have worried. The monkeys weren't interested in him. They just wanted to enjoy their newfound freedom. They scrambled into the trees and swung between the branches as if they were remembering, for the first time in years, the acrobatic possibilities of their arms, legs and tails.

Ben was just about to run to the next Portakabin when he heard the distinctive sound of footsteps.

Ben didn't know much about monkeys. Till yesterday, he hadn't even known the difference between them and apes. But he was sure about one thing: they didn't wear shoes. Which meant someone was coming and it was time for him to hide. He dodged round the Portakabin.

He waited there for a moment, then his curiosity overcame his caution, and he poked his head around the side of the wall.

Mrs Skinner was hurrying between the Portakabins, looking through the open doors, and staring at the monkeys in the trees. She looked as if she'd got dressed in a hurry. She was wearing black wellies, a woollen skirt and a big baggy jumper. Her hair was all over the place. Tucked under her arm, she was carrying a gun.

Ben dodged back round the side of the Portakabin. He didn't like the sight of that gun. It was a shotgun, not a rifle. A blast from that would pepper you with pellets. And maybe even blow your head off.

He thought through his options. He could run. He could hide. He could try to invent a story to explain his presence in the camp. Or he could. . .

Yes, he thought. That's what I'll do.

He reached into his pocket and grabbed his phone.

There was no signal, but that didn't matter. Ben went through the menus till he reached the alarm. He set it for one minute in the future, then turned the volume to full.

He sneaked another look across the grass.

Mrs Skinner wasn't far away, but she had her back to Ben. She was looking at the monkeys in the trees. She must have been wondering how they got there.

Ben took two quick paces and reached the Portakabin's open door. He tossed the phone inside. It landed on a pile of straw. Ben dodged out of the doorway and ducked back round the corner, hoping he hadn't been seen.

41

It was the longest minute of Ben's life. He didn't count the seconds. He just stood very still, trying not to make any noise and willing time to pass as fast as possible. He could hear the sound of footsteps on the grass. He wasn't sure if Mrs Skinner was coming closer or going further away. There was nothing he could do. If she came round the corner, he'd just have to run, hoping he had enough time to get away before she shot him.

The alarm went off.

It sounded very loud to Ben. He hoped it did to Mrs Skinner too.

He heard her footsteps. She was coming closer. Then the sound changed. Now she was walking on wooden boards rather than mud and grass. She had gone through the door and stepped into the Portakabin, searching for the source of the noise.

Ben knew if he stopped and thought about what

he had to do next, he wouldn't be able to do it, so he just forced himself to start moving. He ran round the side of the Portakabin. There was no sign of Mrs Skinner. He slammed the door. He heard a shout. He pulled the bolt, locking the door. There was another shout. Yes! She was trapped! He had caught her in her own cage.

Ben hurried across the grass towards the next Portakabin. He hadn't taken more than three or four paces when a loud voice stopped him.

"Ben!"

He turned round.

Mrs Skinner was staring at him through the Portakabin's window, her fingers clasping the wire mesh. "Let me tell you something," she said. "Monkeys are very dangerous little animals. Do you know that?"

"I'm not scared of them," said Ben.

"You don't have to be. They're not going to hurt you. You're bigger than them and they don't attack anyone who's bigger than them. But what if they attacked your little sister?"

"She can look after herself," said Ben.

"Babies can't look after themselves. What if one of these monkeys went into the village and bit a baby in its pram? How would you feel then?"

Ben didn't know how to answer that question.

"I think you'd feel bad," said Mrs Skinner. "You'd feel guilty. You wouldn't want a baby to get a big bite taken out of its face, would you?"

"No," said Ben.

"That's why you have to be careful with monkeys. You can't just let them run around the place. They're vicious creatures. They'll attack someone. I've seen it happen. I can understand why you want to free them, Ben. You think they're cute. Well, they are. I think they're cute too. But that doesn't stop them being dangerous. Do you understand what I'm saying?"

"Yes," said Ben.

"You've made your point," said Mrs Skinner. "Now, let's get them back in their cages before they do any damage. Will you help me do that? Will you let me out?"

"I don't know," said Ben.

"We'll pretend this never happened. You won't be punished, I promise you won't. Why don't you just open the door and we'll talk about this like grown-ups?"

"I suppose I could."

"Of course you could. Come on, open the door."

"I will," said Ben. "If you tell me something."

242

"I'll tell you anything," said Mrs Skinner. "What do you want to know?"

"Where's the lion?"

"Which lion?"

Ben described the roaring that he and Kitkat had heard in the woods.

Mrs Skinner smiled. "You'd be surprised how many people make that mistake. That wasn't a lion. That was a howler monkey."

"There isn't a lion?"

"I wouldn't be walking round here if we'd lost a lion," said Mrs Skinner. "No, that was just another monkey. Right, Ben, I've answered your question. Fair's fair. Will you open the door and let me out of here?"

Ben shook his head slowly from side to side. "I can't do that."

"Why not?"

"I've got to let the other monkeys out first."

"We had an agreement. You said you'd let me out if I told you about the lion."

"I lied," said Ben. He turned his back on Mrs Skinner and hurried towards the next Portakabin.

He had only taken a few steps when a voice shouted after him.

"Stop! Or I'll shoot!"

Ben stopped.

"Turn round," said Mrs Skinner.

Very slowly, Ben turned round.

Mrs Skinner was holding the shotgun to her shoulder. The end of the barrels were poking through the wire mesh, aimed at Ben. "Come back here," said Mrs Skinner.

"If you shot me," said Ben, "you'd go to prison."

"Not for killing a thief."

"I'm not a thief."

"You're on my land." Mrs Skinner smiled. "Come back here, Ben. Open the door. You know it's the right thing to do."

She was a good shot, Ben knew that, and would never miss him from such close range. She'd pepper his legs with pellets. Or blow his head off.

He noticed one of the monkeys. It was sitting on the Portakabin, directly above Mrs Skinner's head. It looked small and skinny and, somehow, very happy.

"I don't think you'd really shoot me," said Ben.

"Yes, I would."

"I don't think you will." He turned his back on Mrs Skinner and walked towards the next Portakabin.

Behind him, he could hear the sound of her voice: "Ben! Don't be an idiot!"

He ignored her.

"Let me out!" Her voice got louder and more desperate. "Stop right there!"

Ben walked onward, waiting for the shot.

He knew he would feel it before he heard it and he could already imagine exactly what it would feel like. A fist crashing into his back. He would be thrown forward. The pellets would pierce his flesh like a hundred skewers.

He would lie on the ground, shuddering and crying, but no one would come and help him. The blood would drain slowly out of his body till he was dead.

He kept walking, but the shot never came.

42

Ben reached the next Portakabin, pulled the bolts and opened the door, then hurried onward. His monkey followed him. And others did too. They could have swung themselves into the trees and hidden in the woods, but they chose to stay in the camp, watching as Ben freed more monkeys from their prisons.

He could hear Mrs Skinner shouting to her sons. "Jacob! Fred! Jaaaacccoob! Heeeelp!"

He knew he had to hurry. Even if the two men couldn't hear her now, they'd soon come to see what was taking their mother so long.

He ran from Portakabin to Portakabin, pulling the bolts and opening the doors, then moving onward, leaving the monkeys to take their first nervous steps into the open air.

Some of the monkeys seemed to be frightened of freedom. They preferred what they knew. They stayed inside their Portakabins, staring at the open doors, not daring to grab what they were offered. Others were braver. They lunged forward before the door had even fully opened and hurled themselves through the gap, springing into the crisp, clean air. They dodged past Ben, scampered across the grass and swung themselves into the trees.

Ben would have liked to stop and watch them, but he knew he didn't have any time to waste.

Mrs Skinner's voice grew quieter and less distinct, disappearing behind the sounds of monkeys celebrating their freedom. They shrieked and squealed, hissed and growled, giggled and howled, cooed and twittered, the chorus of extraordinary noises getting louder as more monkeys joined the party. If Ben had heard them but been unable to see them, he'd never have guessed what they were.

Ben didn't know how many he had released. Eighty? A hundred? Maybe even more. The numbers didn't really matter. The only important thing was getting them out. He was determined to keep going till he had freed every monkey in the camp.

He headed back in the direction that he had

come, unlocking the Portakabins that he had previously ignored when he was searching for the strawberry thief.

He was followed by an army of monkeys. He didn't know why. If he had been confined in a small, dark Portakabin and then unexpectedly released, he would have put as much distance as possible between himself and the species who had locked him up. But these monkeys felt differently. They danced through the trees and rolled on the grass, stretching their limbs and testing their strength, but never let Ben out of their sight.

He had almost reached the last of the Portakabins when he saw a tall, thin man hurrying towards him. It was Jacob Skinner. He was carrying his rifle.

Ben looked around.

There was nowhere to hide.

Should he run? No, he couldn't outrun a grown man. Let alone a bullet.

He stood still, his arms by his sides, waiting for Jacob to reach him.

Jacob was dressed in jeans and a green jacket. He looked tired, grumpy and dishevelled, as if he'd just got out bed, which he probably had. He stopped opposite Ben and said, "You've done it this time. You're in serious trouble." Jacob Skinner gestured at the monkeys in the trees. "Those are ours. You can't just walk off with them. Don't you understand that?"

"Your mother wants to see you," said Ben.

"How do you know?"

"She told me."

"Where is she?"

"Over there." Ben waved vaguely in the direction where he had left Mrs Skinner.

Jacob wasn't convinced. He grabbed Ben's arm. "You'd better come with me. Let's call the police, see what they say."

"Wait," said Ben. "Listen."

They stood still and listened, but the only sound was the chatter of monkeys in the neighbouring trees. Jacob tightened his grip on Ben's arm. "I'm not going to be fooled by you twice." He whirled Ben round and led him in the direction of the farm. "Is it you who's done the computers too?"

"Which computers?" said Ben.

"They've all gone crazy. Is that your doing?"

"What's happened to them?"

"I don't know. They're a mystery to me, computers. But my brother's on the phone to some chap in India, trying to mend them. What have you done to them?"

"Nothing," said Ben.

"You can talk to Fred. He'll know the right questions to ask. You can tell him what—"

"Sh!" interrupted Ben. "Listen!"

"Stop telling me what to do!"

"Sorry. But can't you hear it?"

"Hear what?"

Ben didn't answer. He just waited for the noise to be repeated.

And there it was.

This time, they both heard the distant sound of a human voice shouting at the top of its range.

"JAAAACOB!"

Immediately Jacob released Ben's arm. "Is that her?"

"Of course it is. Like I said, she wants to see you."

"Is she hurt?"

"I don't know."

Jacob stared in the direction of the voice, trying to work out exactly where it was coming from, then glanced at Ben. "You'd better wait here," he said. "Don't go anywhere."

"I won't. I promise."

"Good lad." Jacob sprinted in the direction of Mrs Skinner's voice.

Ben waited for a moment, watching him go, then hurried in the opposite direction. It was the third time in a day that he'd broken a promise. Oh, well. He didn't care. Unlike his sisters, he thought there were more important things in life than telling the truth.

He ran across the grass, followed by a hundred monkeys.

43

For a long time, nothing happened. The room was quiet. Kitkat lay on the top bunk and fell asleep. Harmony did some yoga, stretching her arms, twisting her legs, contorting her body into strange and unnatural shapes. Frank sat on the lower bunk and stared at his computer.

In one corner of the screen, he had placed a small box showing whatever footage was being transmitted from the camp's cameras. The box was empty. The cameras were still dead. In another corner of the screen, he was checking message boards, seeing what had happened since he posted messages to them last night. He was glad to see that his posts had already got a lot of attention.

He had converted some of the footage from the cameras into still pictures and posted them to message boards where people gathered to discuss animal rights issues. He didn't know much about the subject himself, but that didn't matter. He pretended he did. He wrote short messages to accompany each photo, explaining that the pictures came from a farm, but not where it was. He had promised to reveal that information in the morning.

He now wrote a few emails, giving the precise location of the farm and making suggestions for what people might like to do next. For each of the emails, he used a different account, so they couldn't be traced back to him.

He was halfway through writing another email when, without any warning, the cameras came back on.

Frank alerted the others, then started work.

Harmony and Kitkat huddled round the laptop, staring at the footage and watching what he was doing.

Frank tried to switch the cameras off again, blocking their transmission, but he couldn't break into the system. Someone had changed the password. He had been locked out. Given enough time, he would have been able to sneak past their defences and crack the password again, but that would have taken hours, even days. He couldn't do anything quickly enough to help Ben.

He sat back, admitting defeat.

Harmony said, "What do we do now?"

"I suppose it's time for plan B," said Frank.

"What is plan B?"

"We don't have one."

For a few moments, no one said anything. They stared at the computer, wondering what to do next.

The screen showed a peaceful view. Trees were moving gently in the breeze. Early-morning sunlight lit up the lush grass. The only signs of humanity were the fence and the Portakabins, but there wasn't a single person to be seen.

"Where's Ben?" said Kitkat.

"I can't see him," said Frank. "He must be there somewhere."

"Let's look for him."

"Sure," said Frank. He pressed a key repeatedly on the computer, switching the view from camera to camera, moving all around the camp, watching what was happening. He took them along the fence, around the farm and into the Portakabins. From every perspective, things looked much the same: it was a quiet, peaceful morning and nobody seemed to have got up yet.

"Go back," said Kitkat.

"Why?"

"I saw something. Go back to the last one."

Frank pressed a key. The picture on the screen changed. They were looking through the lens of a camera pointed at a Portakabin.

"There's nothing," said Frank.

"Exactly," said Kitkat.

"What do you mean?"

"Look." Kitkat pointed at the screen.

The others hunched forward, peering at the live footage streamed directly from the camp, but they couldn't see anything interesting.

Frank said, "What am I meant to be looking at?"

"The door's open," said Kitkat.

"So?"

"So where are the monkeys?"

Frank smiled. He pressed a key, changing views, looking through a different camera at another Portakabin. It was exactly the same. The door was open and the interior appeared to be empty. He moved around the camp, looking at different views through different cameras, and his smile grew wider. Kitkat was right. Someone had opened the doors of all the Portakabins. The monkeys had gone.

Harmony said, "But where's Ben?"

"I guess he's with the monkeys," said Frank.

"And where are they?"

"Don't ask me."

"He must be coming back," said Kitkat. "Let's go and wait for him."

Frank switched off his computer. They left the room, closing the door behind them. If Jennifer got up, she'd assume that the children were sleeping late. They tiptoed downstairs, grabbed their shoes and went outside. The girls crouched on the ground to tie their laces. Frank hissed, "I've forgotten something."

He ran back inside.

Harmony and Kitkat waited on the porch, swinging their arms to keep warm. The sun had climbed higher into the sky, bathing the garden in a warm glow, but the air was still chilly.

A minute later, Frank returned. He was carrying two white sheets bundled in his arms.

Harmony said, "Where did you get those?"

"From my bed," said Frank. "And Ben's."

"What do you need them for?"

"You'll see," said Frank. "Come on, let's go."

Harmony wanted to question him further, but she decided not to bother. She was beginning to understand how Frank worked. If you let him do his own thing, he usually came up with pretty good ideas.

They hurried across the lawn and down the lane.

44

Ben ran through the woods. He could hear the sounds of monkeys crashing through the trees above him. He hoped his own monkey, the strawberry thief, was among them, but he didn't have time to stop and check. By now, Jacob must have unlocked the Portakabin and released Mrs Skinner. Ben was breathless and exhausted, but the thought of the Skinners, mother and son, him with his rifle, her with the shotgun, made him run even faster.

He sprinted across the quarry. He could have stopped and hidden in the caves, but decided it would be better to try and get home.

On the other side of the clearing, he could see the high brick wall that separated him from safety. But he wasn't home yet. Nor was he alone. There were three squat shapes sitting in a row on the top of the wall. Who were they? The Skinners? Or monkeys who had sped ahead and got there first? Or. . .? Yes! As he came closer, he recognized his sister, his half-sister and his stepbrother.

Ben plunged through the nettles, pursued by his army of monkeys. Some had disappeared into the forest and others had lingered in the quarry, but he still had the loyal support of fifty or sixty. They scrambled through the nettles behind him or swung in the trees above him, following him wherever he went.

Ben stood at the base of the wall, surrounded by monkeys, and looked up at his siblings.

Harmony, Kitkat and Frank might have been perched precariously on the top of a wall, looking down at a long drop, but they looked as comfortable as if they were relaxing in big leather armchairs.

"Hello, bro," said Kitkat. "I see you've finally found some friends."

"Very funny," said Ben. He wasn't in the mood for jokes. He was breathless, exhausted and scared. Any minute now, Jacob and Mrs Skinner might appear on the edge of the forest, shooting anything that moved. He said, "It's very nice of you to come and meet me, but how am I supposed to get up there?"

"You'll need this." Frank lowered down a long white rope.

As Ben reached for the end of the rope, he realized it was actually a sheet.

Frank had torn the sheets into long, thin strips and tied them together, making a rope. Jennifer would be furious, but she was going to be cross about so many things that the loss of two old sheets wouldn't make much difference.

Frank, Harmony and Kitkat climbed down the ladder and stood in the road, holding one end of the rope, counterbalancing Ben's weight as he hauled himself up. Anyone who drove down the road would have seen them, but luckily no one was passing at that time of the morning.

Step by step, hand over hand, he climbed the wall. His feet scrabbled against the bricks. The sheet groaned and creaked, threatening to rip in half. He balanced on the top for a second, then scrambled easily down the ladder and joined his siblings in the road.

Kitkat opened the gate. Harmony bundled the sheets into her arms. Frank and Ben carried the ladder. They hurried home.

Many of the monkeys had stayed in the quarry and the woods, and many more had lingered in the road or on the wall, enjoying their newfound freedom, so only about twenty accompanied the children up the lane. Some of those stopped to inspect the trees. Others searched for food in the undergrowth. By the time that they arrived at Quarryman's Cottage, the army of monkeys had dwindled to a little troop of just half a dozen. Of them, only the strawberry thief had been here before, but he must have told the others what to expect, because all six swarmed straight across the garden, scaled the fence, dodged the barbed wire and threw themselves into the strawberry beds.

Ben, Harmony, Frank and Kitkat ran across the grass and pushed through the gate. They were just in time to see six happy monkeys starting their feast, cramming pawfuls of strawberries into their mouths. Juice ran down their chins, dripping on to their furry bellies. They looked as if they hadn't eaten so well for months.

Their cries of joy must have alerted all the other monkeys within earshot. Almost immediately, two more descended from the trees and came to join them. Another hopped over the fence. One wandered through the gate as if he'd happened to be passing and had come to see what all the fuss was about.

As the number of monkeys increased, so did the volume of their shrieks and squeals, attracting yet more. They dived down from the trees and plunged into the strawberries, eating whatever they could find.

One of the monkeys lifted his head and looked around the vegetable garden till his eyes met Ben's.

They stared at one another.

Ben remembered the moment that he had first seen this monkey and how amazed he had been. Only a couple of days had passed since then, but watching twenty monkeys plunder the garden now seemed completely normal.

He could see a kind of signal in the monkey's eyes, a recognition that they knew one another, and something else too, although he wasn't sure what. Was the monkey trying to communicate? If so, what did he want to say? "Hello." Or: "Thanks for getting us out of there." Or even: "Why don't you join in? These strawberries are delicious."

After a few seconds, the monkey must have remembered that he didn't have any time to waste, because he tore his eyes away from Ben's and dived down into the bushes, delving under the spreading leaves with both paws.

He'd have to be quick. More monkeys were arriving every minute. The garden was packed. They clambered up bamboo poles, grabbed runner beans, clustered around the tomatoes, dug up potatoes and swarmed over the fruit cage, rattling the wire mesh.

Inside, they could see bushes laden with fruit, but they couldn't reach it. The mesh had such small holes that they couldn't squeeze their paws through. They shook the wire, jumped on the roof and bashed the sides, howling with frustration.

The fruit cage swayed and creaked. It had been built to withstand a few birds, not an army of angry monkeys. Pretty soon, the whole structure was going to collapse.

One of the monkeys soon worked out how to unlock the latch on the door. He yanked it open and leaped inside. For a few seconds, he had the whole cage to himself. His eyes gleamed. His paws moved fast. He stuffed fruit into his mouth, grabbing as much as he could while he had the chance.

One of the others saw what he'd done. He scrambled down from the roof and joined him. More did too. They poured through the doorway, packing every scrap of space inside the cage.

Monkeys sprawled across the bushes, feasting on blackberries, raspberries and redcurrants.

All Ben's attention was focused on the monkeys. He'd never seen anything so fascinating. Which was why he didn't even notice when someone else came into the garden.

45

Ben might not have seen the woman coming through the gate, but the monkeys did. They were constantly alert to the possibility of danger. As soon as another human being entered the garden, they stopped whatever they were doing and turned to look at her.

They could have scampered over the fence and taken shelter in the trees, but none of them wanted to relinquish the fruit in their paws. Some hadn't eaten so well for months. Others had never tasted such fabulous flavours. Having spent their entire lives in captivity, they'd never had the chance to eat a fresh wild strawberry and they weren't going to give it up without a struggle. They stayed very still, standing or squatting exactly where they were, staring at the woman who had come into the garden, waiting to see what she did next. Perhaps she was harmless and they could continue stuffing themselves on blackberries, raspberries and redcurrants. But if she showed any sign of wanting to hurt them, they would flee.

Ben followed the monkeys' gaze and saw Mrs Skinner.

Harmony, Frank and Kitkat saw her too.

None of them knew what to do. They didn't speak. They didn't even move. They sat as still as the monkeys.

Mrs Skinner smiled at the children and said, "Good morning."

No, it's not, thought Ben. It was before. But it stopped being good as soon as you got here.

He looked at the gun tucked under Mrs Skinner's right arm. She had swapped her shotgun for a high-powered rifle with telescopic sights. It was the same type of rifle that Jacob had previously used to tranquillize the strawberry thief.

Ben realized that he'd been an idiot. He shouldn't have come back to Quarryman's Cottage. Mrs Skinner had been to the cottage before. She must have guessed that this was where Ben would bring the monkeys.

If he'd had any sense, he would have taken them deep into the woods, miles from anywhere, and hidden them where they wouldn't be found. Instead, he'd led them into a trap.

What could he do?

Mrs Skinner wouldn't be able to shoot every monkey. Not with one gun. She'd only have time to bag a few before the noise scared the others away. Ben hoped the strawberry thief would be one of the lucky ones.

How could he help? Should he distract Mrs Skinner's attention? Argue with her? Grab her gun? Or just jump to his feet, wave his arms and shout, trying to scare the monkeys away?

Before Ben could decide what to do, Mrs Skinner fixed her eyes on him. "You're in a lot of trouble," she said.

"So are you," said Ben.

"Me? Why?"

"For locking up all these monkeys."

"I've done nothing wrong," said Mrs Skinner. "All the authorities know exactly what's happening at Hunchback Farm. We've been inspected. We've got certificates. We're strictly legal. You're the only one who's broken the law."

"You torture monkeys," said Ben. "That can't be legal."

"I don't torture them. I farm them. There's a big difference."

"It looks like torture to me."

"That's because you know nothing about farming. You live in the city. You're not one of those vegetarians, are you?"

"No."

"Do you eat eggs?"

"Yes."

"And chickens?"

"Yes."

"Why don't you take a trip to a chicken farm? See how they're kept. Compared to chickens, my monkeys are living in a holiday camp."

"Monkeys are different to chickens," said Ben.

"What's the difference? They're all animals, aren't they?"

Ben wasn't sure how to reply to that. Of course monkeys and chickens were both animals. So were humans. Did that mean it was right to eat humans? Or wrong to eat chickens? Were some animals better than others? If he really cared about the monkeys, should he become a vegetarian? And if he wasn't a vegetarian, how could he complain about the treatment of the monkeys?

Mrs Skinner smiled. She understood Ben's silence to mean that she had won the argument. "I think it's time to take my monkeys back home." She called out, "Jacob! Jacob! In here!"

A moment later, Jacob Skinner stepped into the vegetable garden and stood beside his mother. He was holding his own rifle. He scowled at the four children, then lifted his rifle to his shoulder and took aim at one of the monkeys in the strawberry beds.

"Not yet," said Mrs Skinner. "Get those ones first." She pointed to the other end of the vegetable garden. "Go and shut the door. Lock them in the fruit cage. Don't let them out."

"I won't," said Jacob.

Ben and the others watched helplessly as Jacob walked across the vegetable garden to the fruit cage, shut the door and fastened the latch, locking all the monkeys inside. They screeched and chattered at him, clinging to the walls and roof, searching for a way out, but they couldn't escape. They were trapped.

Jacob nodded to his mother. "All done," he said.

"Good lad," said Mrs Skinner. "Now, pick yourself a target. We can't get them all. They'll be off as soon as we start shooting. Nothing we can do about that. Just try to get as many as you can."

"Yes, Mum," said Jacob. He raised his rifle, pointed at one of the monkeys in the strawberry bed and prepared to fire.

Mrs Skinner said, "You ready?"

"Yes, Mum."

"Wait for my word," said Mrs Skinner.

Fingers tightened on triggers.

Mrs Skinner said, "And f—"

But before a single shot could be fired, a voice echoed across the garden.

"Stop!"

46

Jennifer had been woken by the monkeys. Mistaking the noise for the dawn chorus, she turned over and tried to go back to sleep. When she heard a car coming up the lane, she realized something was wrong. She jumped out of bed, grabbed her slippers and hurried downstairs.

Some people would have felt uncomfortable to find themselves standing in front of an old woman, a young man, four children and a hundred monkeys, wearing nothing but a white cotton nightie and a pair of pink furry slippers.

Not Jennifer.

She didn't feel a moment's embarrassment. She stood tall, her nightie billowing in the breeze, and took a long, slow look around the vegetable garden, almost as if she was enjoying the attention. Her eyes rested on the children for a moment, then swept over Mrs Skinner and Jacob and the monkeys and the fruit cage and what remained of the strawberries. When she had seen everything, she turned her attention back to Mrs Skinner and said, "What on earth do you think you're doing?"

"Good morning, Mrs Fitzroy." Mrs Skinner smiled. It was a smile without a trace of warmth. "I've come to collect my monkeys."

"These are yours?"

"They are indeed."

"All of them?"

"Every one. And, if you don't mind, I'd like to take them home."

"I'm afraid I do mind," said Jennifer.

"What do you mean?"

"This is private property. You have no right to be here. Nor do you have any right to fire a gun here without asking my permission first. I'd like you to leave, please."

Mrs Skinner pointed at the monkeys in the trees, the fruit cage and the vegetable garden. "Those are private property too. Your children have no right to steal them."

"What do you mean, *steal*? What are you talking about?"

"Your son isn't just a trespasser, Mrs Fitzroy. He's a thief too. He's committed a serious crime. But we

271

can deal with him later. First, I want my monkeys back."

"You're not going to shoot them," said Jennifer. "Not if they're in my garden."

"How else am I going to get them back?"

"I don't know," said Jennifer. Her tone made it quite clear that she didn't care either.

"Tranquillizers don't hurt them," said Mrs Skinner. "You've already seen that for yourself. Why don't you take your children inside and let us get on with our job?"

"We're not going anywhere," said Jennifer.

"Are you saying I can't have my own property?"

Jennifer smiled. Her smile was as cold as Mrs Skinner's had been. "That's exactly what I'm saying."

"You're not giving me much choice, Mrs Fitzroy. I'm going to have to call the police."

"What a very good idea," said Jennifer. "Let's ring them now."

47

Ben refused to leave the monkeys with the Skinners and Mrs Skinner refused to leave the monkeys with Ben, so Jennifer suggested that everyone went into the house together. She led Mrs Skinner inside, followed by Harmony, Frank and Kitkat.

Ben and Jacob came last, each of them suspiciously watching the other.

They left the garden in the hands of a hundred happy monkeys, who searched through the raspberry bushes and the strawberry beds, hunting for any uneaten fruit.

The kitchen felt very cramped with seven people inside. There weren't enough chairs and no one knew what to say.

Jennifer rang the local police station. She had only been talking for a few seconds, explaining what had happened and asking for a police car to come to the cottage as soon as possible, when confusion clouded her face. She said, "I'm sorry, I have no idea what you're talking about. You'll have to explain it again. Who are these people?" She paused, listening to the policeman on the other end of the line, then said, "Would you like a word with her? No, no, you needn't bother. She's right here. I'll pass you over."

Jennifer offered the phone to Mrs Skinner. "They'd like to talk to you."

"I'd like to talk to them too," said Mrs Skinner. She snatched the phone from Jennifer's hand. "Hello, this is Hermione Skinner. I'd like to report a theft." She listened for a moment, then said, "Who told you that?"

She listened for a little while longer and asked a few more questions, then said, "Yes, I'll be there. I'll see you in a minute. Goodbye." She switched off the phone.

Jennifer said, "What did the police say?"

Mrs Skinner was deep in thought. She didn't appear to have heard the question.

Jennifer said, "Mrs Skinner, are the police on their way?"

Ignoring her again, Mrs Skinner rang another number and put the phone to her ear. "Hello, Fred.

It's me. I know, I've just spoken to the police. Yes, they told me. Is it true?"

As she listened to his response, her frown deepened into a grimace. "That doesn't make any sense," she said. "Where did they come from?"

Mrs Skinner listened for a little while longer, then said, "I'm coming home. Don't do anything till I get there." She switched off the phone.

Jennifer said, "Would you mind telling me what's going on?"

For the third time, Mrs Skinner ignored Jennifer. She turned her attention instead to the four children. In a low, angry voice, she said, "Did you do this?"

Ben answered for all of them. "Did we do what?"

"Are you responsible for these photographs?"

"What photographs?"

"My son just told me that photographs of the monkeys have appeared on the internet. The first ones were found last night. Others have appeared this morning. Messages too. Emails. Stirring up trouble. Saying all kinds of terrible lies about me and my family and our farm. Encouraging trespassers and protesters. There are animal rights people standing outside the gates to the farm. Fifty of them. And more on their way. Hundreds. Maybe thousands. From all over the country. That's what the police told me. But I don't understand. How did you do this?"

"I didn't," said Ben.

"Don't lie to me."

"I'm not lying. I didn't do it."

"Someone must have." Mrs Skinner took two steps forward. Her hands were trembling with fury. "You probably think this is funny. Let me tell you, it is not funny. It is not clever. It is not good or wise. This is my family! My farm! How could you do this to me?"

"I haven't done anything to you," said Ben.

"Then who did?"

"Me," said Frank.

Everyone turned to look at him.

Frank had a small smile on his face, as if he had blown up a whoopie cushion and placed it on a chair that someone was just about to sit on.

Mrs Skinner said, "I hope you're pleased with yourself."

"I am," said Frank. "I've saved the lives of a hundred monkeys."

"I'll get them back again," said Mrs Skinner. "By this time tomorrow, every one of those monkeys will be in their cages."

"They won't," said Ben.

"Oh yes they will," said Mrs Skinner. "Come on, Jacob. We're going home. We're needed at the farm."

She marched to the door, not bothering to say any final parting words to Jennifer or the children.

Jacob scurried after her.

Ben followed them. He didn't trust the Skinners. He wanted to escort them to their car, down the lane and away from Quarryman's Cottage. He had a feeling they might try to snatch a few of the monkeys to take home with them.

He needn't have worried. The Skinners jogged across the grass and clambered into their Land Rover without even glancing into the vegetable garden. They had forgotten all about the monkeys. They had more important things to think about.

Ben stood outside the house and watched them go. He was soon joined by Harmony, Kitkat, Frank and Jennifer.

Mrs Skinner drove. The Land Rover jumped forward, skidded across the lawn, tearing deep tyre tracks in the grass, and accelerated down the lane.

When the noise of the engine had faded, replaced by the singing of birds in the trees and the chattering of monkeys in the strawberry beds,

Jennifer looked at the four children and said, "Which of you wants to tell me what's been going on?"

Ben, Kitkat, Harmony and Frank glanced at one another. None of them said a word but, by some kind of unspoken agreement, they decided that Ben should be the one to talk.

He told Jennifer everything. She asked a few questions, but mostly she just listened and let him speak. He explained how he had woken himself at dawn, tiptoed out of the house, climbed over the wall and sneaked into Hunchback Farm. He described the Portakabins packed with monkeys and the conditions that they were forced to live in.

He had found a monkey farm, he said, where the monkeys spent their entire lives in tiny, cramped cages. He didn't know why the Skinners were breeding them and he didn't really care. All that mattered was the monkeys. They needed to be rescued. He hadn't originally intended to release more than one, but when he saw what was being done to them, he had suddenly understood what he had to do. He couldn't just save one of them. Or two. Or five or ten. He had to rescue them all.

"You really shouldn't have done that yourself,"

said Jennifer. "Even if you see someone acting like a criminal, you don't have any right to take the law into your hands. It's very dangerous. And it's illegal. You should have called the police."

"They wouldn't have believed me," said Ben.

"Then you should have told me."

"You wouldn't have believed me either."

"Of course I would."

"But I did tell you. And you didn't believe me."

"That's not true," said Jennifer. Then her face changed. "Oh, Benjy. You did, didn't you?"

Ben nodded.

Jennifer sighed. "I don't really know what to say. You must hate me."

"I don't," said Ben.

"Am I a terrible mother?"

"Don't worry, Mum. You're fine."

"Are you ever going to be able to forgive me?"

"I've forgiven you already."

48

Harmony rang the RSPCA and told them that a hundred monkeys were sunbathing in the vegetable garden. The person on the other end of the line just laughed.

"I'm not joking," said Harmony. "You'd better send someone quickly. They've already eaten all the strawberries and I think they're getting restless."

An hour later, a van arrived. An RSPCA warden got out, took one look at the monkeys and rang for reinforcements.

The RSPCA spent the rest of the day in the cottage, the garden and the woods, offering snacks to the monkeys, trying to persuade them to come down from the trees.

Ben didn't want to watch.

He knew the RSCPA were doing the right thing. He was sure they wouldn't be cruel. And, although he didn't know where they would eventually take the monkeys, he felt confident they would find a clean, secure home for them, somewhere far better than the farm. Even so, he didn't want to see the monkeys losing their freedom.

He would have liked to say goodbye to the strawberry thief, but he couldn't bear to watch him being shot by a transquillizer dart or fooled by a handful of tasty food, then shoved in the back of a van. One day, he thought, we'll see one another again. In a jungle, perhaps. Or even a zoo. But not here. Not now.

Ben stood by the gate at the end of the lane, watching the procession of people and vehicles heading down the road that led to Hunchback Farm. There were bicycles and mopeds, cars and trucks, and even a double-decker bus with an enormous rainbow painted on its side.

As the day went on, more and more demonstrators joined the protests. They came from miles around. Some carried placards and banners. Others shouted slogans through loudspeakers. Many more simply walked in silence, adding their presence to the protest against the monkey farm.

As they walked past the gate, they chatted with

Ben, asking if they were going the right way. Some gave him a leaflet or a badge. Others invited him to join them.

A small, shabby-looking man stopped by the gate. He was carrying a notebook. He said to Ben, "Do you live here?"

"No, I'm just on holiday."

"But you've been staying here?"

"Yes."

"You must have seen some interesting things."

"Not really, no."

"You haven't seen any of these monkeys?"

"Monkeys? Here? Why would there be monkeys in the middle of the countryside?"

"That's a good question. If I find the answer, you'll be the first to know. See you later."

"Bye," said Ben.

The shabby man hurried into the road and started a conversation with one of the animal rights activists, asking where she had come from and what she was doing here.

Throughout the day, more journalists came down the road, armed with notebooks, recorders, microphones and cameras, writing stories for newspapers or filming footage for the evening news. Everyone knew about the photographs on the internet, but no one could discover who had been the first to put them there.

Someone suggested that they must have been leaked by a disillusioned employee who wanted to expose what was happening inside the farm. The story spread and soon everyone was repeating the same facts as if they were the truth, explaining that the employee had chosen to keep his identity secret because he didn't want to be prosecuted.

That night, the story was featured on news broadcasts on every channel.

Some reports said that the farm had been completely legal. Others claimed that all kinds of laws had been broken.

Some said that the government was involved and the monkeys would have been used for military experiments on poison gases. Others said that new vaccines would have been tested on the monkeys and, without them, doctors couldn't discover whether medicines actually worked.

By the following morning, the truth had come out.

The Skinners had owned Hunchback Farm for many years, but they could no longer make enough money from regular farming, so they started breeding monkeys instead.

They farmed monkeys as if they were chickens, sheep or pigs. When the monkeys were fully grown, Mrs Skinner sold them to drug companies, who used them to test new products.

A week ago, they were transferring some of the monkeys out of their cages so they could be taken from the farm to a laboratory on the other side of the country. When the monkeys had been loaded on to a truck, the driver went to the toilet before his long drive, leaving the cages unattended. One of the monkeys managed to unlock the latch. He opened the door and fled, followed by the others.

Most of them were found within an hour or two. They had simply sat in the trees around the farm, not really knowing what else to do with themselves. Years of captivity had made them stupid. Others stayed free for a day or two. The strawberry thief lasted the longest. He was the most cunning and intelligent of all the monkeys – and the only one who managed to find his own food.

When Ben and Kitkat met Jacob in the woods, he had been looking for lost monkeys. Just like them, he was chasing the strawberry thief.

*

One of the Skinners' clients was a large pharmaceutical company. Their spokesman was interviewed on the news.

"We have a legal responsibility to ensure that our products are safe," he said. "That's why we test all our products rigorously before selling them to the public. Animal testing is sometimes a necessary part of this process. But we are, of course, utterly committed to ensuring that all animals are treated as humanely as possible. Many of our customers have expressed their concerns about the alleged conditions at Hunchback Farm and we are going to mount a full-scale investigation of what has happened. However, before we see the results of this investigation, I can already tell you two things. Firstly, we are going to terminate our contract with the farm. Secondly, every one of the monkeys will be found a new, safe and comfortable home."

They kept their word. Within a week, the monkeys had been taken to zoos and sanctuaries around the country.

Ben would have liked to take the strawberry thief back to London, but he knew it was cruel to keep monkeys as pets.

Instead, the strawberry thief went to a sanctuary in Dorset, where he would live with a group of capuchins in a large, airy cage. It wasn't the same as being free, but it was a lot better than spending every hour of the day and night in a small, dark, overcrowded Portakabin.

When the manager of the sanctuary came to Hunchback Farm to collect his monkeys, he came to Quarryman's Cottage too and thanked Ben for all he had done.

The manager brought some pictures of the sanctuary. Ben studied them carefully and quizzed him about the conditions. He wanted to know all the details of the strawberry thief's new home: where he would live, what he would eat, how he would exercise, who he would share his cage with and what he would do all day to prevent himself going mad with boredom.

The manager was a quiet, serious man. He answered every question carefully and intelligently. By the end of their conversation, Ben had decided that the sanctuary was the best possible place for the monkey to spend the rest of his life.

The manager promised that Ben could come and visit whenever he wanted.

"I will," said Ben. "And every time I visit, I'm going to bring him a big bag of strawberries."

49

They watched the empty tracks, searching for the first signs of the 10.18 to Bristol.

Halfway down the platform, a white cat was stretched out on a wooden bench, fast asleep. Passengers glanced at their watches and shifted impatiently from foot to foot, wondering how late the train was going to be.

Ben, Harmony, Frank and Kitkat were back in the small railway station where they had met a couple of weeks ago. Jennifer had already said goodbye to Frank in the carpark and was now sitting in the car, typing on her laptop, working on the final chapters of her book.

The four of them had been waiting there for several minutes when Kitkat said, "You know what? We need a name."

The others looked at her. None of them knew what she was talking about.

Ben was the first to speak. He said, "What sort of name?"

"To call ourselves," said Kitkat.

"I'm happy with my own name, thanks."

"No, not you. Or me. We need a name for all of us."

"Why?" said Frank.

"Because we do," said Kitkat, sounding so sure of herself that none of the others dared disagree.

They tried to think of a name for themselves.

"What's wrong with the Amises?" said Harmony.

Kitkat shook her head. "Only two of us are called Amis."

"Then the Fitzroys," suggested Ben.

"Don't be silly," said Kitkat. "That's just as bad. Only two of us are called Fitzroy."

"If you want to call us anything," said Harmony, "why not just call us the Amises and the Fitzroys? Because that's who we are."

"That's too long," said Kitkat. "And too complicated. Can't you think of anything better?"

"No," said Harmony, shrugging her shoulders. "Sorry."

Ben scratched his head.

Frank looked at his phone and checked the time.

Kitkat closed her eyes and tried to think.

They stood in silence for a minute or two.

A guard walked along the platform.

A couple of passengers hurried through the ticket barrier and glanced at the electronic display, checking to see if the train had already been and gone.

The white cat woke up, rolled over and went back to sleep.

"I've got it," said Kitkat.

The others looked at her.

Kitkat waited for a moment, till she was sure that she had their full attention, and then she smiled. "The Misfitz," she said.

"The what?" said Ben.

"We're half Amis and half Fitzroy," explained Kitkat. "So we're the Misfitz. Don't you see? It's perfect! That's what we should call ourselves."

"I'm not sure," said Frank.

"I don't like it," said Ben, shaking his head. "It sounds stupid."

"We don't even need a name," said Harmony. "We're perfectly happy how we are."

"Oh," said Kitkat. "OK."

She folded her arms, turned her head and stared along the tracks, hoping none of the others could see her expression. She didn't want them to know how upset she was.

A moment later, they heard the distant sound of the engine, speeding towards the station.

Frank hoisted his rucksack on to his shoulders and slid his arms through the straps.

The train emerged from the trees, eased down the platform and shuddered to a halt. Doors swung open and passengers stepped out.

"I'd better get going," said Frank.

It was a small station and only a few fast trains came through each day. If you missed one, you'd have to wait hours for the next.

Ben, Harmony and Kitkat walked Frank to the door of the train, then took turns saying goodbye.

Kitkat went first. She wrapped her arms around her brother and squeezed as hard as she could. "Bye, big bro."

"Ow," said Frank. "That hurts."

Kitkat giggled and squeezed even harder. "Be good."

"Don't worry, I'm always good."

Kitkat released him and Harmony stepped forward. She kissed Frank on both cheeks, then hugged him too. "Have a nice trip home. Say hello to your mum from us."

290

"Sure."

"We'll see you again soon, won't we?"

"Maybe at Christmas," said Frank.

"Definitely at Christmas," said Harmony. "But we'd like to see you before then. Why don't you come to London for a weekend? Wouldn't that be fun?"

"I guess," said Frank.

Now it was Ben's turn.

He didn't want to hug Frank or kiss him. He could see that Frank wasn't too keen on hugging or kissing either. They could have shaken hands, but both of them would have felt stupid doing that, as if they were pretending to be older than they actually were. Not knowing what else to do, they simply stood awkwardly opposite one another, each of them waiting for the other to make the first move.

If the train hadn't been about to leave, they probably would have stood there for hours, but Frank knew he had to get on, so he said, "Bye."

"Bye," said Ben. "Have fun in Bristol."

"Thanks. Come and stay if you want." Frank looked at the girls. "You too. All of you."

"Yes, please," said Kitkat.

"That would be great," said Harmony.

Frank hesitated, as if he wanted to say something else, then changed his mind and stepped into the train.

Kitkat shouted after him, "Don't forget your lunch!"

Frank turned round.

Kitkat handed him a small plastic bag. She had packed it herself earlier that morning, filling it with two cheese sandwiches, a tomato, an apple, some chocolate and a piece of Harmony's famous flapjack.

"Thanks," said Frank. He took the bag. Then he smiled. "The Misfitz," he said. "You know what? I like it."

Before anyone could reply, Frank turned his back on them and headed down the carriage, searching for a seat.

Ben, Harmony and Kitkat walked alongside the train, peering through the windows at their brother, following his progress.

Frank wanted a seat to himself where he could work on his computer without anyone bumping his elbow or peering over his shoulder. Halfway down the carriage, he found what he was looking for. He stuffed his bags on to the overhead luggage rack and tucked his laptop under his arm.

The last doors closed. A whistle blew. The train nudged forward. Ben, Harmony and Kitkat walked alongside, keeping pace with the carriage, then dropping behind as it sped up.

Frank stood by the window, waving to his siblings. They waved back till the train curved around the tracks and they could no longer see him. The noise of the engine faded. The train flickered between the trees and was gone.

"Christmas is five months away," said Kitkat. "I don't want to wait that long. Can't we see him before then?"

"I'm sure we will," said Harmony. "He invited us to stay."

"He didn't really mean it," said Ben.

"Yes, he did," said Kitkat. "Frank always says exactly what he means."

"Come on, you two," said Harmony. "Let's go and find Mum."

She hurried along the platform, heading for the carpark. Kitkat trotted alongside her.

Ben strolled behind them, lost in thought. He wondered how he was going to spend his time now Frank had gone. He had some books to read and a couple of DVDs to watch, but there was nothing else to do. Hours of boredom stretched ahead of him.

Oh, well, he thought. You never know. Something interesting might happen. He jogged along the platform and caught up with his sisters.

Don't miss the next exciting

MISFITZ mystery

Two Tigers on a String

The case of the missing mother

One minute Frank's mum is setting off for work – as usual. The next she's vanished into thin air. The police are baffled. It's up to the Misfitz to search for the clues, and Ben is a brilliant detective . . .

Together, the four Misfitz must skip school without getting caught and travel across the country following the puzzling trail. Their investigations lead them to a mysterious mansion - the home of the Tiger.

Published in September 2009